The Cat and the Queen of Hearts

A Midnight Louie Las Vegas Adventure

Book 2

Other Five Star Titles
by Carole Nelson Douglas:

The Cat and the King of Clubs

looked sun-bleached among the greener leaves of the decorative plantings beloved of architects. The University of Nevada at Las Vegas campus had been hewed from new buildings, community pride, and local benefactors, so small shade trees dotted the landscape as if scattered by a compulsively methodical latter-day Johnny Appleseed.

Yet towering exotically among all this academic order and spanking achievement loomed a few rough-barked pine trees. Several almost brushed the third-floor windows of the Flora Dungan Humanities hall. Inside, the constant drone of the air-conditioner provided a subliminal white noise that never quite competed with Professor Austen's dryly erudite accents, even when he was merely presenting a student writing effort.

It wasn't hard to discern the author of the unusual passages he had just presented to the class. She was the long-limbed, pink-faced young woman at the very back of the room of raked seating, who was even now shrinking onto her tailbone in a futile attempt to escape everyone's attention.

"Now." Professor Austen adjusted his black-framed glasses on his ever-so-slightly aquiline nose, folded his sweater-clad arms—if the weather was too hot for tweed Norfolk jackets, Professor Austen wore cardigan sweaters from Scotland woven from every shade of heather and equipped with leather patches on the elbows—and cleared his throat again.

"An admirable attempt. It shows . . . er, vivid word choices and endless imagination. It also delves into the seedier aspects of life in our city, and on that I would mark it down. Las Vegas as a fleshpot is a cliché, Miss, er . . ." He frowned down at the paper to verify its perpetrator's name. "Miss McGill."

One hand lowered the frames of his glasses as he glanced at the students from under a corrugated forehead, waiting. At last a long, narrow arm slowly rose at the rear. Professor Austen nodded recognition.

"I see Miss McGill anticipated my reaction and took care to situate herself well out of my purview."

The class laughed knowingly. This early in the fall's first semester, classroom camaraderie was nil yet, but would-be writers always made an appreciative audience for the professor's arid brand of humor.

"But." He eased his weight off the desk corner and replaced the paper neatly on a scanty pile. "This is a *creative* writing class. Miss McGill merits an A-minus for creativity—and a D-plus for content. Please, Miss McGill, try to find some other inspiration in Las Vegas besides the tawdry daydreams purveyed by the Strip and Glitter Gulch. You obviously don't have the slightest experience of what you're writing about. The 'Emir of Abba Dhabba's son' indeed."

"Excuse me, Professor, but—"

He turned from selecting a new paper for presentation. "Well, stand up then, so we can hear you. Don't be shy."

After a pause, she slid long legs from under her desk and stood, nearly as tall as her unlikely fictional heroine, a fact not lost on the man at the front of the room.

Unlike the scintillating Sirene, however, Miss McGill was fully clad, in faded blue jeans and a loose, long-sleeved sweatshirt. A pale, makeup-bare face proclaimed her age to be somewhere in the tender twenties.

Professor Austen allowed a smile to touch his sober lips. Wish fulfillment fueled more student fiction than even professors realized. "You wished to rebut me, Miss McGill?"

Her low voice carried despite a tremor of shyness, or rebellion. "Only to say that seventy percent of the people in this city feed their families and build their churches and schools on the money made from the casinos. And they're considered respectable citizens. Why isn't the industry that's the very heart of Las Vegas, both economically and sociologically?"

"Respectable is not synonymous with worthwhile, Miss McGill."

"Nor is it synonymous with good literature," she suddenly shot back, her faced rouging with embarrassment as everyone turned to stare. "Look at Damon Runyon, he wrote about the people on Broadway in the twenties and thirties, the gamblers and petty criminals, the chorus girls—"

"Yes, yes. But that's light entertainment, not serious fiction. Or do you consider your story serious fiction?"

"No, I would never claim—"

"But I'm being unfair, a prediliction among college instructors, I'm told." He smiled with charming modesty at his students in general before returning his attention to the student in particular. "Obviously, you're serious about your writing. Perhaps that's the best definition of serious fiction. But you need to find a larger subject matter to be serious about."

"What? Death and taxes? War and revolution?"

Professor Austen removed his glasses, revealing amused gray eyes. "Those subjects sufficed for Tolstoy. Perhaps you should apply yourself to taxes; not much of a literary nature has been written about them." He glanced at the big round schoolhouse clock on the wall.

"The important thing, class, is that Miss McGill *wrote.* She did not waylay me before class to beg off because she hadn't had time to write anything; she did not merely re-

15

phrase some balderdash she read before. She wrote an original short story. And that is where we all must begin.

"So before you snicker, my friends, examine your own consciences. I'd be obliged to see *your* literary attempts by tomorrow. Turn off your MTV stations for an hour and see what you can dream up if you desist being mere passive consumers of a pack of rock musicians' nightmares. That'll be all."

Austen turned back to his papers as the students filed out with their customary hubbub. He didn't face the room again until silence filled its empty seats. When he did look up, he found himself not alone.

She was standing behind him, the long-legged one, as vigilant as a gazelle frozen on an African savanna, her bright hazel eyes calmly watching. He was startled, being unused to regarding female students on his own eye level.

"Yes, Miss McGill? I hope I didn't embarrass you just now. The writing soul is fragile."

"Oh, you probably did, Professor," she admitted wryly, notebooks clutched to her chest. "But it isn't your fault." A grin darted across her gamine features.

He whipped off his glasses to stare at her, then jammed them back on. "That's very kind of you, Miss McGill—to excuse me. Usually I do the excusing."

She smiled again, then her long forefinger speared her paper on his desk. "I thought I typed my name on there."

"You did." He snatched up the papers. "It's right here, Miss McGill."

"Darcy," she interrupted firmly. "If you keep calling me 'Miss McGill' I'll think you dislike me as much as you do my writing."

"Not your writing; that shows definite promise. It's merely the subject matter . . . but if your heart is set on chronicling the sins of Las Vegas, well then, I imagine there are enough sins committed in this benighted city to busy you for some time."

"You imagine?" Her eyebrows, delicately plucked, leaped upward. "Haven't you ever experienced Las Vegas nightlife in the flesh?"

He was stacking his books and arranging his face into the same rigorous order. Was she *teasing* him?

"Hardly, Miss McGill. It's quite possible to live an entire lifetime in this city and completely avoid the excesses of the Strip or Downtown."

"Darcy," she insisted with a warmth that belied her earlier shyness.

"Please believe the 'miss' is no term of dismissal." He smiled. "It's simply not proper for me to address my students on a social level. Now I've got another class elsewhere, so. . . ."

He stopped at the door, taking off his glasses and jamming them in the sweater pocket to regard her with a slightly misty focus.

"Look. If you like writing about chorus queens and sheiks of Araby, go to it. Don't let some stodgy old professor talk you out of it. But don't expect him to like it, either."

"You're not old, Professor." Her eyes were as wide open as the African plains. "Why would you refer to yourself that way?"

He noticed with annoyance that she hadn't disagreed with the "stodgy" part of his self-description. "I'm old enough to have earned a Ph.D., young woman," he said, rather stodgily, reminding himself that even at the ripe old academic age of thirty-two maintaining an unreachable façade could sometimes be damned hard work. "That contributes to aging before one's time. And speaking of time. . . ."

He was squinting pointedly at the functional Timex on his wrist, moving his arm closer and farther by turns. Darcy McGill caught it in her loose, commanding grasp as efficiently as a nurse taking a pulse.

"Three-fifty-five, Professor, time for your next class, The Twentieth-Century English Novel, and time for me to run. 'Bye now."

Darcy darted down the hall as if *he* had been guilty of detaining *her*, rather than vice versa.

Professor Stevenson Eliot Austen shook his head, which was boyishly topped with a rich thicket of mahogany hair. Here and there gleamed a rare silver thread, badges of either Ph.D. travails or genetic inheritance.

"Bizarre girl," he noted to himself, as he was becoming too fond of doing. Shrugging, he preceded to the next classroom with its predictably checkered array of faces blasé and eager.

Darcy McGill slammed her class books down on Van von Rhine's desk.

"Can I dump these here? I never hear the end of it when I bring them into the dressing room, and everybody's always poking and prodding—"

"Go ahead. Just collect them when you're done. I'll leave the office open," promised the dainty blonde woman behind the massive desk, itself massively overrun with paperwork. "How are things at the university campus these days?"

"Oh, ducky!" Darcy hurled her collapsible frame into a chair. "I love creative writing, but the classwork is more personal than I thought it would be. Today the instructor read my assignment—aloud!—in front of the whole class."

"Instructors generally read papers to their classes aloud," Van said.

"Maybe Nicky's right," Darcy went on glumly. "You can learn as much from life as you can in a classroom."

"Of course Nicky's right," Van agreed. "He's my husband—and he has a college degree."

Darcy's tennis shoe kicked idly at the desk, dislodging a large black cat from under the kneehole. "Point taken. If hell-raising Nicky Fontana can be the first in his somewhat larcenous Family to get a sheepskin, I guess I can pin one on my dressing-room door."

"You don't have a dressing-room door. Aren't you sharing the storage area with the other three queens?"

"Yes, and Nicky keeps promising that he'll build some more dressing rooms down there, so we can all have private niches."

"The show's doing better than we thought, which doesn't leave much time for a revamp. Danny Dove knows what he's doing in the matter of revues. We never wanted the Crystal Phoenix to be a major show hotel, it's not nearly as big as the Goliath or the MGM Grand or Caesars."

"It's big enough, Van, to allow you two to polish your fingernails on your respective lapels—oh, yikes! Fingernails! I better get down and start donning my armaments." Darcy waved ten talon-bare fingers as if drying imaginary nail lacquer. "Professor Austen said I had imagination, but I can't dream up crimson claws." She stood with a groan. "And what are you doing working so late, anyway? Nicky won't be crazy about that."

"Nicky needs to have his machismo challenged regularly," Van said, rising to see Darcy to the door.

In the process one stiletto of her Italian heels pinned a swatch of black fur to the floor. A sound like an affronted jackhammer roared through the room.

"Oh, Louie, I'm sorry." Van bent to bestow a solacing caress on the gigantic cat crouched by her feet, then stepped elaborately over him. "He's such a lump of coal; always underfoot. Or maybe I'm just clumsy."

"Clumsy?" Darcy surveyed Van's petite figure. "You're a china shepherdess. You should galumph through life like me, five-feet-eleven and still growing."

"But you dance like a sugar plum fairy, all froth and meringue. Being tall is an advantage on a Las Vegas stage, Darcy. Girls the country over would kill to be in your tap shoes."

"Especially at the Crystal Phoenix, where the haute high rollers all come. You've done a great job managing the place, Van. If Nicky hadn't married you, I bet his uncle Mario would have, just to get such prime talent in the 'Family.' I gotta admit they sure can see me from the back row, or *in* the back row. I gotta go, or it'll be curtains—and I won't be ready."

Darcy sprinted out of Van's office and past a row of ancillary cubbyholes to the hotel lobby, which opened up before her like a peony, so lush it seemed about to collapse under its own weight. A yellow-white blaze of crystal chandeliers poured light down on a rich navy-and-burgundy tapestry below.

Against this elegant background, people thronged around the casino tables and slot machines like ants heading for the hills of home. Dice rolled, Plexiglas shims pushed greenbacks into below-table slots, quarters and house coins clanked down the greedy stainless steel throats of endless rows of slot machines.

None of this interested Darcy, who darted through a nondescript door and down a wide, well-lighted hall. She waved a greeting to the guard who sat eating peanuts at the stage door entrance and galloped down a set of steep stairs.

She shrugged past protruding wall pegs hung with glittering shields of costumes battle-ready for their owners to rush by and don them.

She dashed through a pair of twelve-feet-high double doors to the storage area she shared with three other dancers and threw herself down at her allotted spot.

Dusty makeup lights bordered the memorabilia stuck into the mirror-frame edges like prom cards into a high school girl's bedroom bureau looking-glass. Dancers were examples of arrested social development, a critic had once said, and there was some justice to the remark, Darcy often thought.

Since she had been ten, Darcy had haunted dance studios and practiced pliés until she thought her knees would snap. She was inured to dressing room chaos, knotted muscles, and sweat-soaked leotards.

She had dreamed her Ohio girlhood away on toe shoes and her own reflection in walls of wavy mirror. She had always wanted to be a professional dancer. And now she was.

Darcy smiled at the odd way dreams have of ending and stuck more bobby pins into her daytime knot of soft brown hair. In minutes the lotion-and-powder-spattered square of mirror before her reflected a smooth expanse of pancake makeup emphasizing the exaggerated, painted-on features needed to be seen on stage—soot-lined eyes, arched black eyebrows, blue-shadowed eyelids, lips glossed redder than a candied apple. Topping it off were jet-black false eyelashes long and stiff enough to do double duty as chimney sweepers' brooms.

She looked exactly as she had described Sirene. *Fictional indeed,* she fumed. *Write about what you know. Mularkey!* She *had* written about what she knew, and Professor Austen hadn't believed her. He seemed determined to see her as some nice tall girl in the back row of his classroom when Darcy secretly longed for a much flashier place, front and center, in his attentions.

Her mind painted his features over hers in the mirror. She knew them by heart—stream-cool gray eyes that could warm in a second, a slow smile that was the velvet glove worn over his steely professional classroom demeanor. Darcy longed to shatter that professorial air of slight formality. She'd love to see Stevenson Eliot Austen with his hair rumpled, his rep tie loosened, his jacket and feelings unbuttoned—Reality intervened.

Face it, Darcy told the painted lady in the mirror that she often wished she had the nerve to be in her own right, instead of just donning her as a nightly stage persona. *You'd love to see Stevenson Eliot Austen come completely unglued— over Darcy McGill*

Darcy stood frozen at the front of the classroom, books clutched to her chest, flattening her bosom to pancake state, and stared deeply into Professor Austen's sincere gray eyes. She swallowed, hard.

"After your next class?" she repeated like the town idiot. "To . . . talk?"

"I wasn't inviting you to an execution, Miss McGill." Austen paused in arranging the books upon his desk in their usual fastidious order. "Would waiting around campus for an hour cause a problem?"

"No. Yes! I have to be somewhere by six."

"This won't take long—say, ten minutes? We can meet here. No one's using the lecture hall, and you could kill time by writing in your journal." He nodded to the poison-green-notebook supporting Darcy's textbooks in her cradling arms, and smiled in what could be described as a kindly fashion.

It made no difference. Darcy walked as one condemned to the back row and slipped into her usual seat.

"Why does Mr. Chipps want to see you after class?" hissed a lanky American Lit major who aspired to be an Off-Off-Broadway playwright.

"I, uh, don't know. Maybe he didn't like my last assignment, as usual."

"Relax, Darcy," Ashley Rhee, a Korean student advised.

The advice was appreciated, but the giver was so porcelain and petite that she made Darcy feel that she stuck out as much as the five-story plaster figure of Goliath outside the fabulously tasteless Strip hotel of the same name.

Darcy ran nervous fingers over the acid-green notebook cover. Professor Austen was quoting something from the Cavalier poets that put goosebumps on Darcy's shoulders, when a zillion BTUs of air-conditioning couldn't do as much on the stage of the Crystal Phoenix.

She gnawed a thumbnail before hastily tearing the finger from her mouth. If she didn't leave something to build on, her false nails would never stick tonight . . . oh, Lord, she was going to be late! Even ten minutes would put her behind schedule. Why hadn't she just said so? Why hadn't she just said *no?*

When her classmates drained from the room at the hour's end, Darcy remained high and dry in her seat. Below her, Professor Austen glanced up with a quick smile, more reminder than courtesy, before leaving for his next class.

Darcy stayed put. Once she opened the green notebook, but her private words looked unbearably public under glaring fluorescent lights. Darcy watched the big round clock on the wall, and how the fringed pine branches outside the window fanned the blue afternoon blaze of desert sky. She started to write that observation down, then another.

"I hope I'm not interrupting you."

Had time gone that quickly? Darcy looked up, then down. Professor Austen stood in the doorway, his arms empty of books for once, empty of everything but a slim furl of papers—hers.

"No. I just finished." She scrambled to put away her papers, grabbed her purse, and began descending the aisle stairs while he waited. They seemed eight hundred feet long, and the risers felt impossible narrow. Maybe one of her low heels would catch on a riser and hurl her down, into his arms—

But nothing dramatic happened, except that she arrived at floor level and eye to eye with Professor Austen, who seemed particularly intimidating today.

Perhaps it was the Norfolk jacket, Darcy told herself. Too tweedy. He always got stuffier when he wore a Norfolk jacket. It was the sort of English-y thing one would expect Dr. Watson to wear when accompanying Holmes on a case in the boondocks.

"Don't look so panic-stricken, Miss McGill. I only want a few words. Have a chair."

She sat in the molded plastic model he drew up to his desk.

"I see you took my advice to keep your subject matter if you felt like it." His eyes were skimming the tops of several assignments. "And your writing is sharpening. In fact, they make quite an amusing set, these adventures of the sumptuous Sirene."

He actually produced a twinkle behind the intervening lenses. "Miss McGill, I hope you won't take this in the wrong way—you're a talented writer with an astute eye for detail—but I'd be derelict if I didn't. . . ."

"Didn't what?"

"Advise you to give up these imaginative excursions into the sleazy side of life in Las Vegas! What can you know of it, anyway?"

"I've lived here half my life. I went to high school here, I—"

"Living in Las Vegas gives no insight into life in the fast lane," he objected. "There are two cities here—the ordinary, quiet, churchgoing community that would exist quite nicely without the gaudy goings-on that occur on the bright side of town. Then there's 'Las Vegas'—the flashy, no-holds-barred city that panders to greed and ignorance, that glamorizes gamblers and chorus girls, high rollers and hookers—really, these are not admirable people, Miss McGill. I hate to see a talented young woman like yourself losing her head in candy-floss dreams of an unreal world."

"I'm not *that* young! And I guess I can lose my head if I want to." Darcy felt stung to hear her very way of life dismissed so glibly.

"You're young enough to know nothing of the world that attracts you," Austen continued with calm, infuriating certainty. "A cardinal rule of writing is to write what you know—"

"I know! And I *am!*" Darcy burst out.

He actually reared back, as if to see her in better focus.

"I know about everything I put in those papers! I *was* writing from life."

"Not *your* life?"

His eyes were shocked now. Darcy felt an abrupt surge of, oddly enough, protectiveness. Would his regard for her "talent" shatter if he knew she made her living as a chorus girl, and liked it? Where was the sweet, unpretentious Darcy he saw in class every week when she needed her? Her anger segued into improvisation.

"Oh. Not *my* life, really. No, it's . . . my . . . my sister's!"

"Oh." His relieved look seemed to justify her wild story. "Your *sister* is one of these"—he paged rapidly through the pages, finding the quote—"these 'hard-working hoofers with hearts as soft as the cherished pink tulle tutus they wore at age nine'?"

Darcy gulped. "Perhaps I exaggerate a bit. Poetic license, you know. But, but Sirene is my sister, yes."

He frowned. "Your parents named you Darcy and her Sirene?"

"Noooo." It did sound unlikely. Darcy's lively imagination cast about frantically. "My parents named her—Irene! But when she went on the stage, she added the *S* . . . so she would stand out."

"I should think that a woman six feet tall would have no problem doing that in a normal occupation and with her right name." He glanced quickly at Darcy, and his dry manner softened. "I'm sorry. I don't mean to imply that being a tall woman is—"

"It is!" Darcy said tersely.

He cleared his throat. "Tell me about your sister. I may put down her profession, but you obviously look up to her."

"Or would if I could." Darcy grinned wickedly, starting to enjoy her impromptu creative fiction. "But we are *exactly* the same height. In fact, we're huh, twins . . . Fraternal twins. Sirene is older by five minutes."

"I see." He leaned back in his wooden swivel chair. "And you went to school together?"

"Of course." She was beginning to believe her own scenario as she sketched it. It was more like a class writing exercise than a lie, she told herself, like composing an entire

Sirene story on the spur of the moment.

"Oh, you should have seen Sirene in high school!" Darcy rambled on. "She was captain of the cheerleading squad, and went out with the star basketball players, and always got the best solos at the dance recitals."

"You didn't dance yourself?"

"Who me? Heavens no! I was the bookish type. Sedate. Sedentary. A little clumsy. I couldn't make it across the classroom to dust the erasers for the teachers without tripping. I was born with three left feet. But Sirene—"

"Yes, I've seen you move around here, and I think I have a sufficiently complete picture of Sirene right here." He patted the papers. "It's you I'm interested in."

"You are?" Darcy gazed into his gray eyes, feeling dazed.

"Of course I'm interested in you. You're far too modest. You're a promising writer, but isn't that sense of humor you volley about like a tennis ball simply camouflage for a more serious side of Darcy McGill? Write your tales of the chorus line, if you must, since they are apparently based on reality of a sort. But I still think you should look beyond them."

"All right."

She stood, a glint in her eyes. Somewhere in that stodgy, professorial speech she had seen that her hero wore more than reading glasses. He had on blinders as big as a billboard. As long as he peered at the world through thick prejudice-tinted lenses, he'd never see or appreciate Darcy as a complete person—chorus girl *and* nice girl, dancer *and* writer. He couldn't even accept her *writing* about backstage life. What made him think that he was so right and she was so wrong? Her Irish temper was up and racing its motor. Talk about stereotypes! How she'd love to teach Professor Austen that the life of a Las Vegas showgirl was not the hollow, clichéd existence he assumed it to be.

He aligned her papers with a smart rap to the glass desktop and slipped them into a wide-mawed leather briefcase.

"I hope you don't have to spend all your weekend reading our little class exercise, Professor," Darcy remarked.

"No way." He smiled amiably, almost rakishly. "In fact, I'm partying tonight."

"Oh." Her visions of a sequestered, studious life into which she could pour the sunshine of her spirit evaporated. "Well, I'm going to kick up my heels tonight myself," she said airily.

"Good! Glad to hear it." His expression warmed with the first flush of personal interest Darcy had detected. "That's the spirit. Can't sit in a corner and write all the time, you know."

"I'll think about what you said, Professor—about being serious." As he took off his glasses, she found herself cataloging the fascinating fogscape of his seriously short-sighted eyes: *Inner quicksilver shifting through a stormy sea-change....*

"Good." He stared at her for a moment as if he too were noticing that eyes could be drowned in. Then he blinked and redonned the glasses like a transparent shield. "By all means, consider being serious, Miss McGill. Goodbye, then, and have a, um, good weekend. Don't stay up too late," he joked, beginning to back away.

"No," she answered, grinning like an accomplished liar. "I won't." But Sirene surely would.

Darcy set off down the long hall, dreading the clogged rush-hour traffic, even if the distance between the university's halls of ivy and the Strip's halls of hilarity and high-kicks were only a few blocks.

Stevenson Eliot Austen was right about one thing, she thought, it was best not to live in a dream world, even if he had been the best thing in it. He was right about another thing, she thought, sighing softly. Two different worlds abided cheek by jowl in Vegas—one giddy and loud, the other placid and quiet—even though some law of physics said that two bodies couldn't occupy the same space at the same time. Somehow Las Vegas the family town and "Vegas" the Sin City did. For the first time, Darcy saw both sides and felt torn between the two.

♥ Chapter Two ♥

"Ooh-la-la, honey! You're late."

One of the doors tall enough to admit an elephant suddenly cracked ajar, and in that crack floated a face as plain as Darcy's had been twenty minutes before.

"Hi, Midge. You're later." Darcy turned in her chair to greet the woman poised in the doorway. "Sit down and stay awhile."

"Funny." Midge sprung her lean, mean, blue-jeaned body into the adjacent chair. "I thought you were worried about being late, and here you beat us all."

"Just fast on my feet," Darcy sang back, executing a series of tap steps with her tennis shoes, still sitting. Darcy grinned at Midge in the mirror before bending to pull off her shoes.

Midge was lean where Darcy was lithe, angular where she was simply supple, and nearly twice her age, although no one was impolite enough to inquire what that might be. Midge's hair hung shoulder-length, Clairol jet-black, and her nose turned down where Darcy's tipped up. Like many dancers, Midge suffered from a characteristic physiological quirk; her chin receded ever so slightly.

Darcy's chin—and everything else about her—was just right. So the Three Bears, a trio of delinquent Chicago halfbacks on a Vegas toot, had assured her once in this very dressing room. Darcy was not about to argue with an inebriated middle lineman, nor was Jake the doorman about to eject three wildly happy halfbacks who'd barged backstage after the ten o'clock show.

made such headway in this once-noble occupation as to be able to say two words, "keep out," in seventy-four. I believe this is what the economists today call "inflation."

Well, I cannot fault so sweet a little doll as Miss Darcy McGill, although she is no little doll in person, as most hoofers in this town start at five-feet-seven. The best and most beautiful average between five-ten and six-one, much like quarterbacks.

Being more than somewhat small in stature myself, comparatively speaking, you can see that a guy like me is handicapped. You can also apprehend that many guys in Vegas come up somewhat short when it comes down to escorting a genuine showgirl about town and not looking like a Dachshund out for a stroll with an afghan (the canine, that is, not the comforter).

Sad to say, the hard-working chorus girl, who asks nothing more of life than a little glitter and good glue for her false eyelashes, is often left at loose ends socially, unless she is unlucky enough to be courted by the bozos who believe that a fat wallet is enough to make up for thinning self-esteem.

So I am very sympathetic to these terpsichorean dolls, who hoof their little hearts out for what amounts to decent pay but not enough to write home about, much less send. Although most tourists regard them as glamorous, Midnight Louie has pounded enough neon-soaked pavements in this town to know that most of these elongated little dolls are ladies whose dreams took a detour. Instead of essaying "Swan Lake" at the ballet, they are shedding swan's-down from costumes that leave little to the imagination but pneumonia.

Still, it is a living, and I am hardly one to quibble. These dolls and myself are soul-mates of a sort, being largely unappreciated in our own times, and I make sure to favor them all with frequent dressing-room visitations. I am especially welcome in the four queens' quarters, known as "the Forbidden Zone" among the other chorusters since the penning of aforesaid verse.

Miss Midge Mancini keeps a wire brush—originally intended for suede shoes, I believe—with which to polish the more hirsute portions of my anatomy. The Misses Trish Reilly and Jo Hastings manage to import caviar of an adequate grade and the occasional tin of sardines for the jolly little pre-show parties we five share.

And Miss Darcy McGill, who has a heart of solid platinum, provides me with a red velvet pillow near the warm rays of her makeup lights and leaves me occasional reading material for the long hours I must while away guarding the below-stage area while everybody else is tapping and rapping in the spotlights upstairs.

It is a lonely and arduous life I lead, but somebody has to do it.

♥ Chapter Four ♥

"Shy? How can a man with a cleft in his chin be shy?" Midge demanded.

"Well, that fits," Jo put in with a frown that barely cracked her pancake makeup. "Listen here: 'pockets broadcasting the fragrance of pipe tobacco . . .' Pipe smokers are always shy."

"Maybe that's because nobody wants to be around them." Trish paused in filing her false nails to wrinkle her nose until her freckles threatened to pop through her pancake.

"Well, somebody must want to be around this one, or she wouldn't bother to write down his vital statistics—'Six feet-plus just right,' with 'eyes gray as smoke and quiet as summer rain.' This guy sounds like a weather report."

"Jo! Where did you get that notebook?"

Darcy was standing indignantly in the doorway, her gym bag dropped at her feet, her hands pugnaciously propped on her hips.

Trish's T-strapped dancing shoe prodded the tote bag near her makeup chair that Darcy often left behind overnight. "Gee, Darce, what're you so mad for? Midge noticed it falling out of your bag. Maybe the cat tipped it over. We just picked it up after the cat was out of the bag." The others giggled with guilty unease at Trish's elaborate innocent act.

"I bet!" Darcy stalked over to Jo's broad and quite bare back. She presented a demanding hand. "Give that back. It's class work."

"Class work. . . ." Jo milked the words into an elongated

incantation of doubt while she held the notebook at arm's length, an unretrievable distance from Darcy. Jo's long false eyelashes rolled ceilingward like a pair of expiring caterpillars. "Class work wasn't like this in my day, girls. What does describing men in this drooling manner have to do with class work?"

Darcy hopped forward on one quick foot to snatch the tablet from Jo's fire-engine-red talons. One of her own normal-length fingernails jabbed the open pages.

"You can see the title right here—'Sketch.' We were supposed to work on physical descriptions for next time."

"Oh, good work," Trish noted with a toss of her heavy red hair. "There's nothing better than getting physical."

"I shouldn't have left it here," Darcy fussed while sticking the notebook back in her bag and pulling her makeup front and center on the dressing table. "But I like to use between-show time to jot some things down. Don't blame the cat, poor baby. You three are more curious than kittens. My writing is private, like this dressing room. So hands off!"

"Oh, she's blushing, girls. Her writing must be very private," Trish purred.

"Yes, it is! Nobody wants people to see things they've written before they're ready to be read. And maybe they never will be. It's like . . . spying."

"Maybe it is." Midge's voice had suddenly grown serious. "Look, Darcy, we were just having a little fun. I guess we had no right to go flipping through your workbook. Sorry."

"That's all right." But Darcy's eyes remained lowered as she savagely sponged theatrical makeup on her face, erasing the angry flush that covered it.

"We're sorry," Jo iterated. "None of us could write her

way out of a paper bag. We didn't mean to make fun of your writing. We just thought you had a secret love."

"And that's okay to make fun of?"

Blonde, red, and black eyebrows raised to consult each other in concert. Midge, being the eldest, took the others' silent lead.

"Hey, I know all the big writers are supposed to be sensitive, but this is ridiculous. We shouldn't have read your notebook. We won't do it again."

Darcy sighed and threw down her sponge. "I'm sorry, too, for being so sticky about it. It's just that my creative writing papers haven't been getting the greatest reception. Maybe I don't know what I'm doing, and maybe I don't even know what I want to do with my life."

"Don't you want to hoof your way to happiness, like the rest of us?" Trish bounded up to perform a sappy soft shoe. "Who the hell knows what we want to do with our lives? I, for one, think it's great you're willing to put the time and money into going to school. We should keep our big mouths shut."

"Right on." "Hip hip hooray." The others seconded her with the enthusiasm of the recently converted.

"Since you're late, can we help with anything?" Midge asked solicitously. "We're all stuck here together in this little room—" They laughed at the obvious contradiction; the storeroom was cavernous. "What I mean is, it's sink or swim. It's up to us to get along or we'll all hang separately—from our G-strings, no doubt."

Darcy broke into laughter and snatched back her rhinestoned version of the skimpy article in question, which Midge had just looped around her own neck to pantomime a hanging.

"Just keep your ersatz claws out of my property, unless

I'm late and need help rounding it up," Darcy advised in mock sternness.

She screamed as a blizzard of pantyhose, makeup sponges, unattached strings of pearls and the ubiquitous rhinestones descended on her.

"Enough already," she pled; concentrating on applying the bright, obvious eyeshadow that had the virtue of looking true blue no matter what shade of tinted gel covered the spotlights. More than one novice chorus girl had experimented with subtle commercial shades only to discover afterwards that lighting changes had transformed her Moonglow Mauve lids into Hideous Bilious Yellow. "If we don't get down to business, I'll be late for my nightly date with destiny."

Van von Rhine, her taffy-smooth baby-blonde hair impeccably rolled into a French twist, her desktop swept clean of paperwork, never looked busy even at her most harried. It was the one trait she could trace to her aristocratic German father, who had managed the top hotels in Europe.

Now, his daughter managed the newest and most daringly marketed hotel in Las Vegas with the same outward orderliness. The fact that she had married the hotel's owner, Nicky Fontana, soon after the Crystal Phoenix had opened the year before, was mere personal frosting on a thoroughly professional cake.

So Van von Rhine looked as cool, controlled and carefree as ever when Darcy bounded into her office the next afternoon.

"Van, I just stopped in to pick up my check, and I wondered—"

Van's eternally composed face altered just enough to advise Darcy of what should have been obvious had she not been in such a rush. A man sat alertly in the leather chair opposite the desk, a man there on business.

"Oh, sorry!" Darcy attempted, uselessly, to shrink against the door jam. "Brenda was away from her desk and I didn't see . . . I'll come back later."

Darcy retreated and, uncertain about closing the door but caught red-handed with her fingers on the knob, compromised by shutting it all but the final foot.

She sunk into a hallway chair. Darcy attacked everyday life like a dancer leaping dramatically onstage and forgetting to look for toe-stubbers first. It often embarrassed her, but the muse of impulse fueled her dancing, as it did her writing.

Politely pretending not to eavesdrop, Darcy strained to pick up conversation from Van's office in hopes of learning just how badly she had blundered.

"Melbourne," the man was saying in an English—no, Australian—accent. Darcy stopped slouching on her rubber spine and leaned nearer the ajar door.

"Your resume is somewhat sketchy, Mr. Smith," Van was responding doubtfully.

"I've traveled a good deal. And I know gambling."

"Somehow I thought so. I must say the international flavor you'd bring to the position is tempting. The Crystal Phoenix views itself as a cosmopolitan hotel, ready to offer the finest in food, accommodations, entertainment and casino gambling. Well . . ." Darcy heard the competent rustle of Van rising from her chair. "I'll let you know."

Murmured thanks and mutual goodbyes followed. Impatiently, Darcy tapped her nervous feet. A man from Melbourne, her lively mind speculated; now what kind of a position would he want?

He was standing beside her as suddenly as if he had produced himself from a hat, a lean, tanned man with a closed face. But his eyes, the palest blue Darcy had ever seen, almost robin's-egg color, were wide open.

He stared at her as if he knew she had overheard every word she could, his narrowing lids and sandy lashes shuttering the odd glimpse of blue. White crow's-feet radiated from the outer corners of his eyes. They could have been laugh lines or they could have come from not wearing sunglasses in the noonday sun around Las Vegas. Darcy read his unreadable face and chose the no-sunglasses theory.

"Darcy."

She had been staring after Van's departing visitor and jumped guiltily before catapulting herself once again into the office.

"Who was the *High Noon* cowboy?"

Startled, Van paused in shuffling some papers into a manila folder.

"Hardly that. The range he rides is the dark of the casino. I'm still trying to set up an experienced staff; he might be our new baccarat referee."

Darcy threw herself into the vacated leather chair. "That kills me, the way they call the house baccarat employees 'referees'—as if gambling had any rules but winning or losing."

"What can I do for you?"

"Oh, sorry, I know you're busy. You've been letting me drop my books off in your office every day. Have you got somewhere safe to stash this?" Darcy waved a spiral-bound notebook with a poison-green cover.

"Does it hold the formula to a new eyelash fixative or the phone number of one of those admiring sheiks of yours, or what?"

"Nothing so intriguing. Just my writing journal for class. The girls were sampling it last night, so I'd rather keep it here and come up between shows to write a bit."

"No problem." Van pulled out a lower drawer on her desk. "Think you'd have any trouble remembering 36-25-36 as a combination?"

"My measurements!" Darcy realized, gawking.

"No, mine," Van corrected dryly. "Nicky's idea. Since we both use the drawer, and boys must be allowed some fun. . . ."

Van smiled at Darcy's carefully neutral expression as she spun the lock shut on the notebook, then came around the desk to see her tall friend out. Van glanced askance at Darcy's well-proportioned but reedy figure.

"What a difference six inches or so make; we don't look at all alike."

"I wish we did," Darcy contributed wistfully at the door.

"Why?" Van asked, astonished.

"You petite, cuddly girls get all the tall men—and the short ones, too. It isn't fair."

"Mr. Smith is single." Van's eyes flicked toward the hall, where the applicant had vanished.

"Forget it! Mr. Flint Steel is not my cup of tea."

"Who is?"

Darcy rolled her impish hazel eyes toward the ceiling as she considered. "Ummm, Nicky isn't too bad—hey, just kidding! No, let's face it. I attract short sheiks and professional flakes."

"Did you ever get rid of that spoiled young man?"

"You mean the emir's son? I hear he finally jetted back to Abba Dhabba with the manicure girl from Caesars, three hundred pair of Italian shoes, the world's largest waterbed and enough unplayed chips to open his own casino. Maybe he'll call it the Sands or the Dunes. . . . Catchy, huh? But he promised to come back," Darcy added direly.

"I hope not. He was more trouble than he was worth, and considering how much he lost, that's saying a lot."

"Speaking of lost, he claims there's a lost camel—or the ghost of a camel—on the desert he wants to find and take back. Along with me. I wonder if he'd ship us back in the same crate?"

Van's vivid blue eyes darkened fretfully as she laid a cautionary hand on Darcy's wrist. "It's not funny. Some of these wealthy Arabs are only oil wells removed from the most primitive kind of sexism. The sad part is they do buy and sell women even today. They were the same in the continental hotels. I hate to see our employees exposed to it."

Darcy shrugged. "You can't stop progress," she said. "Thanks for keeping my girlish secrets safe."

"I don't like it," Nicky said, leaning his head back to stare at a wild black yonder as thick as dotted swiss with midnight stars.

"Hmmm." Van had her head thrown back, too, but her eyes were closed.

A foam of churning bubbles gurgled against their bare shoulders as they sat side by side in the molded fiber glass whirlpool adjacent to their rooftop penthouse apartment atop the Crystal Phoenix. By October the stark Las Vegas summer heat had eased back to put up its feet and cool down. The air temperature was as coddling as a baby's bathwater, and "bliss" was the evening's middle name.

If Nicky Fontana, a vital man whose dark Mediterranean looks played perfect counterpoint to his wife's blondeness, had cared to see artificial night lights, he had only to turn his head and look beyond a rather thorny privacy screen of Mojave yuccas.

There a dimly glittering prow of smoked glass bore a dancing legend of lights endlessly stringing themselves into words like the landmark sign in New York's Times Square. "Nicky Fontana's Crystal Carousel," the small yellow dots of light announced. "Now featuring Mel Torme."

Nicky sighed satisfaction and shut his jet-black eyes. A nearby speaker bubbled with the jazzy serenade of the "Velvet Fog" at his most tactile. Being the owner of a Las Vegas Strip Hotel had its moments. Nicky congratulated himself, for once banning all thought of hotel employees' strikes, air-conditioning breakdowns or irked competitors of his uncle Mario, who tended to take out Family arguments on the hotel belonging to the only absolutely straight Fontana in town.

An ugly thought intruded.

"I don't like it," he repeated.

"You mean that emir's son I was telling you about," Van repeated lazily, "who was after Darcy?"

Nicky shook his head. "That Aussie pit boss. Smith. His employment background is pretty sketchy."

"So's mine," Van retorted.

"Yeah, but . . . 'Sylvester Smith'—come on, if that's his real name, mine's Sal Mineo."

"Some people are given funny first names by their parents," Van said in an injured tone.

Nicky's arm clasped her shoulders just above the bubbles. "I know . . . Vanilla."

"Ooooh!" Her hand slapped a spray of water into his face. "I thought you said you liked my real name. Loved it, you said—"

"I do, I do," Nicky vowed, drawing his wife into a watery

embrace and a series of quick but effective kisses that soon had the thread of their conversation not only knotted but hopelessly soaked as well.

"Well, I'm going to hire him," Van suddenly remarked, much later. "That's my decision as hotel manager. You just own the joint, to quote colorful friends of your acquaintance."

"Okay, but don't say I didn't warn you."

"Anyway, I wish you'd spend more time worrying about your friends than my professional decisions," Van added, pushing herself with difficulty back to her molded underwater recliner.

"Hey, Darcy's your friend now, too. You're really worried about her?"

"Maybe. . . . I don't know, this writing kick is strange. Now she wants to keep her journal locked in my desk drawer during the shows. I don't mind, but—"

"What?"

"Darcy's not what she seems."

"Hey, I question the credentials of some dude from Australia and you tell me it's none of my business; now you're telling me a girl I went to high school with is an imposter!"

"That's not what I'm saying. Everyone thinks that Darcy is Miss Hail Hoofer Well Met—wholesome, happy, slightly daffy Darcy. For all that she prances on your stage letting the tourists ogle her semi-nude form, Mr. Fontana, she's a complex person—and no kid. If she went to high school with you she must be at least twenty-seven or -eight."

"Aghhhh." Nicky suddenly groaned in pain, thrashing as he clapped a hand to his hip.

"What's the matter?" Concerned, Van sat up in the water, completely unconcerned that any star that cared to peek could see more of her than the paying customers saw of Darcy. "Nicky, what is it?"

"My . . . my arthritis," he confessed, breaking into a laugh. " 'At least twenty-eight,' my aching foot! Give me a break, Van."

"That was despicable! I was really worried. It'll be a hot day in heaven before you—"

But Nicky was lunging after her in the water, nothing in the least arthritic about his movements. Shrieks and laughter and droplets of spotlight-silvered spray hurled at the night sky and dissipated into its vast indifference. The stereo speaker poured out its heartfelt liquid vocalizing un-attended. In the spa, whispers and gentle lapping water and extended marital peace negotiations became the order of the evening.

"Turn in our notebooks?"

Darcy sat stunned in her seat the next afternoon, watching her classmates fish the objects under discussion from inside knapsacks and tote bags.

"I—I didn't know he was going to *c-collect* and *read* them," Darcy s-stuttered to the would-be playwright sitting next to her.

He shrugged. "All the better. Old Austen will get a sample of your writing with your hair down."

"He's not old!" she snapped without thinking.

"Hey, it's just a figure of speech. What's the big deal?"

"Nothing." Darcy lingered in her seat while the others filed out.

Each one deposited a notebook on the growing pile atop the professor's desk. Darcy watched them swell as if mesmerized by a spreading mushroom cloud of doom.

Finally, Austen looked up at her, and the green notebook

45724

(clutched in her frozen hands) that she wished she had left in a locked drawer at the Crystal Phoenix. Everyone else was gone. They were alone, utterly alone.

"Saving the best for last?" he suggested. But he sounded eager to read her off-the-cuff scribblings, as if he considered her the best writer in the class.

Darcy rose and slunk down the stairs, her toes stuttering on the risers so that she almost slipped a couple times. For heaven's sake, where was the sure-footed chorus girl when she needed her? Where was Sirene, who knew how to handle everything, including handing your secret heart right into the palm of the man it quivered for?

"Are you sick, Miss McGill?"

"No. Yes! I mean, not physically, exactly." He was looking so damn concerned. And well he should be. If he read what the girls had been thumbing through only a couple nights ago. . . . Darcy cringed, not an easy thing for an almost six-foot-tall woman to do.

"Are you sure you're not ill?"

She nodded, clutching the notebook to her breasts.

"I'm looking forward to seeing your journal," he said encouragingly.

"You can't!"

"Why not?"

"I'm . . . it's not ready."

He straightened, the reluctant authority figure. "I'm sorry. You have to turn it in, it's required."

"But . . . Monday, then." She could write all weekend, create a whole new notebook.

"Everyone else has turned in his or her work today. Why should I make an exception in your case?"

"I didn't know that I had to turn it over," Darcy wailed shamelessly. "You see, I can't."

His lips tightened. "You mean you won't."

"I mean I can't," she answered, her eyes pleading. "I would if I could, but . . ."

His eyes narrowed. "Is this something to do with Sirene?"

"Huh?"

"With your sister Sirene?"

"Oh. With her. Well, yes, actually," she said, playing for time to think. She so hated to disappoint him, but she could never show her face in his class again if he actually read— Darcy shuddered.

"Good God, you really *are* upset. Here, sit down and tell me why. I won't bite."

His hand pressed her shoulder until she sank onto the chair beside his desk.

"It's just that I've never voluntarily shown anyone," she said. That was the whole truth.

"You've sat here and heard me read your rather risqué tales of Sirene to the class," he pointed out. "For crying out loud—"

"But that was finished work."

"I know your notebook efforts might be crude or embarrassing. . . ."

"No, you don't," she muttered. "You don't understand. I *lock* this notebook *up* where I work. I can't let anyone see it."

"You lock it up?" He stared into her eyes, searching for the truth, and found it. "You really are sensitive. What does Sirene have to do with it?"

"Sirene?" *Damn Sirene!* she wished heartily. *Damn all inventions that turn into monsters that turn on their creators.* "Sirene peeked once."

"At your writing?"

Darcy nodded, seeing the scene in her mind now, seeing shy young Darcy—which she had been—and a bolder, brassier version peering over that other Darcy's shoulder. For a second it looked uncannily like . . . herself. "I was—we were—twelve."

"And you kept a journal?"

"Oh, I've always wanted to write," she confessed with absolute honesty. The answering smile in his eyes branded itself on the deepest darkest depths of hers.

"And Sirene violated your journal?" he prompted.

Darcy nodded grateful agreement, happy to have him draw conclusions so she wouldn't have to stretch the truth any further.

"And you can't stand anyone reading your private journals since then, is that it?"

Darcy sighed happily and nodded again, staring into his understanding eyes.

He stared back. Somehow his hand had returned to her shoulder. It felt warm and not heavy at all. Darcy smiled idiotically.

"Do you feel better now, for having told me?" His deep voice hushed a bit, so it vibrated. She almost felt it in his hand.

She could have purred. "Yes, much better. Awfully much better."

"I suppose"—his hand tightened on her shoulder, then abandoned it as he stood and turned away—"I suppose I can make an exception, given the circumstances. Violating a child's privacy can be quite traumatic, even if it's by a sibling."

"A what?" she asked, still dazed by blessed relief.

He wheeled to face her. Darcy was shocked to read anger in his face, an expression she'd never seen there before.

"By your sister! Your damnable sister Sirene! Darcy—Miss McGill, I wish you'd sit back and take another look at your sister, at your relationship. I don't think she's the best influence on you. You really are a bit oversensitive about this—" His fingers paused momentarily on the green notebook cover in her lap, and she jerked as if scalded, whether from what he touched, or where it lay, she couldn't tell.

"You see?" His head shook. "Just try to relax about it. Maybe you could start a journal you know is going to be turned in. Maybe you'll get around your hang-up that way. It's unhealthy to be so . . . secretive . . . about your writing. Just go home this weekend, try to write something you can show me, and don't worry about it."

"You won't flunk me?"

"No." He laughed at the idea.

"You won't . . . hate . . . me?"

"Of course not. My star pupil? I'd have to be crazy. Anyone would have to be crazy to hate you. You've really got to work on a better self-image. What you have to say is important. But you know that, deep down, don't you? That's why you're here in my class."

She stood the notebook securely sandwiched between her arms and chest. "That's why I'm here in your class," she repeated by rote, a dutiful student again.

"Good." He smiled and put on his glasses, then looked at the piled notebooks and sighed. "I've got a weekend of deciphering illegible student chicken-scratchings. I wish yours were among them. It would have given me something to look forward to."

"I—I wish it was too," she said. "I really do!"

And, mortified by her adolescent behavior, she fled the classroom.

♥ Chapter Five ♥

"Dar-cy's got a vis-i-tor, Dar-cy's got a vis-i-tor . . ."

Jo mischievously pranced behind Darcy's chair. Her childish singsong sounded incongruous coming from a woman posing as the black-satin Queen of Clubs and wearing as little clothing as the trey of spades has spots.

She doffed her heavy headdress of fountaining jet plumes to crown Darcy with its dire splendor.

"Guess who it is?" Jo asked coyly.

Darcy froze in unbuckling her red satin T-straps. "Not the Son of the Sheik? Say it isn't so."

"It isn't." Jo tantalizingly produced a mote of yellow paper from the cleft of her bosom, drawing it up between two inverted and barely concealing black satin hearts. "Not unless His Royal Lowness has changed his name to Steven Eliot."

Darcy frowned, mystified.

Jo leaned closer. "Um . . . Austen, I guess, is the last name. I'm afraid the ink smudged from my"—Jo performed a burlesque-style bump that begged for a drum roll—"body heat," she finished in a mock-sexy foghorn whisper.

Darcy snatched for the tiny notepaper, but Jo slapped its glued edge to the litter surrounding Darcy's mirror and retrieved her headdress.

"Cut out the cute and move your fanny, Jo," Midge intervened gruffly. "I'm sure Darcy would rather receive her guest privately."

Darcy, sitting frozen amid the usual post-show chaos caused by assorted chorines changing into street clothes

promoters of a breakfast cereal, Stevenson Eliot Austen read them.

He was smiling by the time he finished. Their homespun humor banished disturbing visions of temptresses in clinging costumes. Even the awesome Sirene was merely making a living during a six-day-a-week grind that was more arduous than it was glamorous. Once removed from this rather bizarre background, he was sure she would sit back sensibly, listen to his advice about her shy twin, then do all within her power to liberate Darcy from a stifling sister worship and put her on the road to academic purity of purpose.

Satisfied with his conclusions, Steven stopped pacing, readjusted his much put-upon glasses, and contemplated a serene future.

Inside the dressing room, a desperate Darcy was pulling open locker after locker. Only five dented and peeling units lurched against one wall and in them the four queens had deposited the shards of what worldly goods seemed essential.

Her own held jeans and a sweater, paperback books, a pair of battered suede boots, an umbrella, and a broken package of sadly decaying Hostess Twinkies.

Jo's wasn't much better. Midge's locker was papered inside with photographs of her kids and her dogs, and held a never-worn makeup smock, a set of electric curlers that didn't work anymore, and six half-empty hair spray cans rusting from the bottom.

The middle locker was jammed with all their junk, which it proceeded to disgorge en masse onto Darcy's tender insteps.

"Ouch! Back, back, I say!" She kicked the effluvia behind

the closing door as she jammed it shut.

Trish's locker was Darcy's penultimate hope. She cracked it cautiously, then sighed vast relief and swung wide the paint-chipped door.

Pristine, hanging quietly as if secreted there by a fairy godmother for a rainy midnight, dangled a single tongue of flame-colored silk. Beneath it, neatly paired, rested red-leather spike heels.

"The answer to a maiden's prayer," Darcy whispered. She extracted the dress and plastered it against herself. "Well, not exactly a maiden, I guess, but . . . it'll do."

She quickly slipped into the dress, which Trish kept primed for sudden hot dates with suddenly hot high rollers. Its short petal-shaped sleeves matched the petal-cut skirt that slit open when she walked. The crossover bodice permitted no bra; the slit skirt allowed for no slip.

Darcy mounted the steep heels and checked the mirror. The ensemble was made for Sirene. It would never have done for Professor Austen to see Sirene in Darcy's undressy denims. An emotion, perhaps shame, knocked discreetly in Darcy's silk-draped breast. Some stronger urge shoved it rudely aside as she surveyed herself in the mirror.

She smiled tigerishly at herself, then darted to the door to sweep it wide.

"I'm ready, Professor!"

"So I see." He peered into the room as if expecting to see witnesses popping out from under the hanging feathers. "I was, ah, just reading the verse on your door."

Sirene's face, stripped of its Queen-of-Hearts excesses but still made up well beyond street wear, stayed as blank as it was meant to look on stage.

"The, um, 'Final Warning.' "

"Oh, that," Darcy's heart leaped like a trapped rabbit's,

but Sirene dismissed the panic. "Darcy scribbled that one day when I complained how everyone was stampeding through this dressing room as if it was the men's room of the *Titanic*."

"I'm sure that a showgirl relishes her privacy as much as the next woman," he conceded. "That's a most attractive outfit," he said by way of uneasy conversation.

"Thanks, Doc." She turned quickly to the mirror for a last primping, the skirt flipping open thigh-high.

The professor looked as if he'd bit his tongue. He tried again.

"I, ah, was perusing the program—"

"You what? Are you sure perusing is legal, honey?" Sirene demanded.

"Reading. I was reading the program and noticed your name is listed oddly. . . ."

Sirene's pliant form froze.

"It says 'R.C. McGill.' "

"That's my real name. Sirene's a nickname."

"So your sister told me." His frown sat his ruggedly refined features even more impressively without the glasses blocking its effectiveness. "But I distinctly remember her saying your real name was Irene."

"Yes!" Sirene spun from the mirror to face him. *Darn that blabbermouth Darcy!* "Ramona Catherine . . . Irene. Irene is my confirmation name."

The professor's sober face brightened. "Confirmation. Glad to hear it."

"Well," Sirene said coyly, "there are more churches in Las Vegas than bawdy houses, did you know that, Professor?"

"No, but it's somehow reassuring, Miss McGill. Now. I suggest we go somewhere quiet where we can discuss your sister, which is what I came here to do."

"What's to say about Darcy? She's as simple as pie. Oh, all right. I know she's your precious student." Sirene elaborately outlined her already red mouth with a swath of Crimson Pirate borrowed from Trish's stash while the professor watched respectfully.

"What d'you say about going to my place?" Sirene suggested, popping up from her chair like an inordinately pleased jack-in-the-box.

"Ah. . . ."

"*Our* place," she reminded him. "There's nowhere quiet in Vegas unless it's private."

"Yes, I can see that, but won't your sister be home?"

"Oh, no." A flash of comet-red fingernails dismissed the idea. "That party's way out in the valley. Darcy'll sleep over."

The professor gaped. "Is she accustomed to doing that sort of thing?"

"Sure. The crowd she hangs out with is from high school. Oh, say, Professor. Don't look so worried." Sirene's fingers captured his chin and shook it admonishingly, her scarlet lips puckered within kissing distance of his as she spelled out the situation. "They're all pals, one big happy family. *Darcy* would never do anything"—Sirene frowned prettily, for once lost for words—"risky?"

He reclaimed his chin by unclamping her long fingers, one by one. "I think you mean 'risqué,' Sirene. And I'm relieved to hear it. So if you'll lead me to your car, I'll find mine and escort you home."

"It's too bad we've both got cars," Sirene reflected, insinuating an arm through his. "Then we could drive together."

"Most unfortunate," Steven said dryly, untangling their limbs. "Look here, Miss McGill, I mean business, and I

70

don't want you to get any ideas otherwise."

"Of course not. Not in a million years," she purred, preceding him through the dressing-room door. She looked back over a silken shoulder. "Just follow me."

♥ Chapter Six ♥

"And to think I could have been quietly playing Japanese Go at the Humanities Department head's house tonight," Steven muttered to himself in front of the plain apartment door.

Sirene, leaning on his arm as her elevated heels seemed to require, delved for the key in a purse that struck him as familiar. She caught him staring at it and promptly lurched against his side, hip-to-hip, the sudden motion unleashing a great deal of what TV marketing experts christen Jiggle.

"Please contain yourself, Miss McGill," he urged, eyeing askance new depths of décolletage.

" 'Miss McGill.' It sounds like an old-maid English teacher," she pouted, opening the door on total darkness. "You *were* calling me Sirene."

He studied the dark uneasily. "You're sure that—?"

"Darcy won't be back till high noon tomorrow, Steven," she assured him with what in fact was becoming the truth. Sirene was becoming her own person. "We can have a nice tat-a-tat. I promise."

"That's 'tête-a-tête.' Um, are there any *lights* in this room?"

"Scads. One right here."

"Where?"

"On the wall behind me."

"Oh."

"Ooooh . . . Steven!"

"Sorry. I, ah, mistook you for the wall. There. That's better."

The sudden brightness found Steven pressing Sirene be-

72

tween himself and the wall in question—how, he could not exactly say. He had nothing in common with this woman, he realized, suddenly horrified by a reaction that had to be purely physical. He was here for a noble purpose. He stepped instantly away to survey the room, and was reassured.

Brick-and-board bookcases, sparse rattan furniture, and profuse hanging plants proclaimed it the usual student domicile. A series of expensively framed prints enlivened the walls above the unpretentious furnishings.

"Very nice," he approved and then frowned, suddenly remembering Sirene's garish tastes.

"Darcy does the decor," she said hastily. "This isn't the kind of thing I go for. It's a little dull."

"Indeed. I think you've put your finger on the root of the problem, Sirene."

"I have?" She vanished behind the kitchen partition but popped her head out a moment later, along with an arm brandishing a bottle of Scotch. "Drink?"

"No!" Settled on the rattan sofa, he reached into his jacket pocket for his pipe, remembered he had left it in his car, studied the area for alternative props, and, finding none, reconsidered. "Well . . . yes."

Sirene shuddered with delight. "I love you eggheads; you make everything sound so important. Straight up or with the rattle of dice?"

It took him a few seconds to interpret her colorful patois. "With ice cubes, please."

She emerged with lowball glasses moments later and handed him the white one with piled ice cubes. "I thought for sure you'd take it without ice, like the English. You look English; you dress English."

"My dear Sirene, I merely teach it."

She draped herself into the chair opposite, a coolie-hat-shaped circle of rattan braced by three spindly wrought-iron legs. The bracing effect of Sirene's sinfully long legs, crossed and bare to where angels dare not tread, was not lost on Steven, who took an even more bracing swallow of Scotch.

"Tell me about yourself," she invited. "Did you always want to be an English professor?"

"Heavens no!" He smiled at his own intensity, then, oddly enough, relaxed. Steven had always guarded his deepest aspirations from his fellow instructors. An academic atmosphere seemed to grade every nuance of ambition. But of course Sirene was light years removed from all that. Sirene wouldn't . . . couldn't . . . judge him. He found himself telling the whole truth.

"I wanted to be a writer," he said. "Then, failing that, I could have settled for simply being a critic and crucifying those who did manage to be writers. But I realized the futility of such an ignoble career, so I decided to do something positive, and teach."

"What kind of books did you want to write?" she asked, her impeccably drawn-on face alive with a look of new interest, looking a little like Darcy lost in the luxury of finding out about her heart's desire. Sirene leaned forward, her hands bracing the glass on her thigh.

"Your, ah . . ."

"Yes?"

"Your . . . glass. It'll leave a moisture ring on that silk."

"Oh, silly me." She rearranged her legs more decorously. "You must be a connoisseur, Doc. Most men can't tell silk from sailcloth," she pointed out slyly. "But what kind of books?" she persisted, her impeccably drawn-on face noncommital.

He cleared his throat. "It's called literary fiction."

"Sounds serious."

"Very serious, indeed. So serious, in fact, that very few writers actually do it."

Sirene nodded seriously, sipping her drink. "I thought all fiction was literary?"

"Well, yes. But some is more literary than others."

"What Darcy does isn't literary?"

"Not in the serious sense."

Sirene nodded sagely. "So you want her to give up doing what she wants to do, so she can do what you gave up on doing a long time ago, is that it?"

"No! Your logic is most . . . convoluted, Sirene."

Her smile widened. "Yeah. I've had guys tell me I'm convoluted before."

He set his drink down on a pile of *Time* magazines and stood to pace out his frustration.

"You seem to be deliberately dodging the point, Sirene. Doesn't Darcy mean anything to you? You share an apartment with her, after all. Don't you see what the very fact of your existence, the mode of your existence, is doing to her self-esteem?"

She waited until his pacing brought him abreast of her and then rose fluidly in front of him, nearly touching him. Their heights were dead even.

He pushed his glasses frame up on his nose again. "You're really quite tall, aren't you? Quite the Amazon. Darcy never seemed—"

"Darcy and I are exactly the same height, Professor. Exactly. Maybe you never looked as hard at Darcy as you're looking at me right now."

"Still . . . you seem taller. As tall as me. I mean—I!"

"Aw, grammar giving you trouble?" She leaned close.

Her hands smoothed his ruffled tweed shoulders. "I'd say I'm just as tall as you. Even Steven."

"It's . . . it's the shoes!" He looked down, hoping to spot the footwear in question.

She lurched suddenly and dropped three inches. "Is this better? Are you feeling less threatened now?" Sirene's uptilted face only drew his down, as quicksand attracts the uncertain traveler.

"That's exactly it!" He thrust her away. "You threaten Darcy."

"Me? Threaten Darcy? Listen, I take good care of the kid. I clue her in on all sorts of things. You'd be surprised what she learns from me."

"But Darcy's no kid, Sirene. Somehow, your mere five minutes' earlier entry into the world gave you an edge, an edge you've been using against Darcy. How old are you?" he demanded from a position on the other side of the sofa.

Lashes long as caterpillars blinked. "Twenty-eight."

He clapped a hand to his forehead in the Del Sarte style famed in melodramas. "How blind I've been! Of course, Darcy's an *adult-ed student,* not just an undergraduate. You see, she's so afraid of competing with you that she passes for a girl instead of a woman."

"Darcy? Afraid of me?"

He took pity on her obvious bewilderment and came around the furniture again.

"I'm afraid so. The only pieces she's turned in for class assignments all revolve around her 'sister, Sirene.' You wouldn't believe the imaginative nonsense she weaves, about you being wooed by the sons of wealthy Arab sheiks and oh—incredible things."

"Incredible, huh?" Sirene's bare foot was tapping, her arms crossed, raising a formidable swell of décolletage.

Steven elected to ignore all that, including the slightly miffed tone in Sirene's voice. He felt himself on the verge of making a breakthrough—that moment when a less agile intelligence is finally led to the inevitable conclusion that he, the instructor, saw all along.

"Don't you see? Your glamorous lifestyle—the clothes, the men, even if most of them are figments of Darcy's imagination. Your rather ostentatious occupation. Even your . . . um, showgirl proportions—all things Darcy has no hope of having. You've intimidated her, Sirene, into becoming a mousy little scholar who pours the dreams she should be living into stories—fantasies—about you."

"Mousy? Little? Darcy?"

"Well, not literally. But figuratively speaking, Darcy can't hold a candle to you in your nightly strut through the spotlights. She's trapped in your glamorous shadow, Sirene, condemned to come second always, expected to be a good sport and laugh at herself and write you a piece of verse to order if you need it."

He knew the warm satisfaction of having convinced her, for Sirene turned suddenly away from him, her fingers fanned atop the coolie-hat chair, her shoulders shaking.

"I didn't know I was such a—a bad influence," she gasped.

Steven considered himself as incompetent to deal with female tears as the next man, but there was no doubt he had caused these and should do something about it.

He approached her gingerly, employing the wise, tolerant tone he applied to distraught D students.

"Now, now." He essayed a small pat on her shoulder. "It's not as bad as that. Knowing what the problem is means you're halfway to solving it."

"Oh, but it *is* bad!" She stood and whirled like a crimson

dust devil, throwing herself against him and burying her face in his tie.

He cast his arms around her to keep them both from toppling.

"It's terrible," she wailed. "I can't help being what I am. I don't mean to make Darcy feel inferior. I never dreamed—"

"There, there." He patted her heaving shoulders again and was rewarded by a slight subsiding. She burrowed into him with a whimper, her temple pressing against his cheek. "I understand that you never suspected your influence on Darcy. And things could be worse. She could have reacted to her inferiority complex by trying to imitate you rather than simply idealizing you."

"That would be worse?" Sirene asked through her hiccups.

"Much worse."

"What's so bad about it?"

"Oh, not that the way you are isn't perfectly splendid for you, Sirene. But it's not right for Darcy."

"Or you," came her smothered voice, followed by further eruptions of an emotional nature under the silky lava of her dress.

"That's not true! I like you . . . quite a bit. You're obviously a very lovely woman. I don't need my glasses to see that. But—"

"Yes?"

"Won't all that makeup run?"

"It's waterproof," she retorted, crushing his lapels with her dagger-ended fingers. "So you think I'm pretty?"

How on earth had the conversation turned to this topic, Steven wondered, but he manfully attempted to deal with it.

"More than pretty," he said as if cajoling a child. "You're—"

"Attractive?"

"I'd say . . . stunning."

"And—?"

"And talented and glamorous . . ."

She looked up, her face surprisingly dry, the makeup unblurred and her expression so luminously expectant, it quite addled him.

Steven's fingers circled on the silk of her back. A scent of Oriental subtlety weaved around him. He couldn't remember when he'd last known a woman who wore perfume this potent—He wished suddenly for his pipe. Or his books. Or even a glass of Scotch three feet away on the cocktail table. But all he had was Sirene, the close, trembling, soft length of her.

"And, and . . ." He fought for words to talk him out of this entrapment, the words that always did. Sirene's ardent eyes stared unblinkingly up at him. He couldn't say what color they were; senses other than sight were surging to the forefront of his awareness.

"And exciting," he said.

She shimmied with pleasure as the word dragged out of his taut throat. Steven felt his hands—as if possessed by their own undeniable autonomy—slide slowly down her back to her hips.

"Soft," his mouth said, drugged by the way the word felt on his lips. She seemed to melt into his bones. "Seductive." Her face strained toward his. The vibration of the words on his lips was searing into his soul. "Sexy." Her crazy eyelashes were lowering like tangled curtains over her eyes so he could finally do what he'd been wanting to do all night.

He leaned his head down the little it took and matched

his lips to hers. This time *he* let the kiss ebb and flow, let it cool and catch fire, soften and then turn to burning steel. Their kiss grew fiercer just before they finally parted.

She took his hand and turned to lead him to the bedroom.

"My glasses—"

"I'll give them back. In the morning."

At the door, which stood ajar, its narrow bar of darkness hinting at delicious secrets-to-be, he threw a last bone to the mongrel of his conscience.

"Darcy."

Sirene smiled tenderly. "She won't be back until long past dawn, lover. And by then, you'll be long gone."

♥ Chapter Seven ♥

The Twelve O'clock Scholar
Speaks His Piece

I consider myself a self-educated individual. Some quite no-table dudes never acquired a sheepskin in their lifetimes, in-cluding Abe the Hat, better known as Mr. Abraham Lincoln, late of Illinois.

You could say I am street-savvy, or that I earn my de-grees in the School of Hard Salami. Everything I am I owe to keeping my peepers primed, my ears pricked, and my mouth sealed tighter than a Sunday school teacher's knees on Saturday night.

I am not the most delicate of guys; many a rough exte-rior hides a heart of Acapulco Gold. (This is a favorite treat of mine, to be found skimming the surface of Mr. Sing Song's personal carp pool in the rear of the Crystal Phoenix, but I am no longer allowed to indulge in this avo-cation, on pain of exchanging a few moments' romp in the pond for a short but fatal stay at the Las Vegas city pound.)

Yet I am a reasonable little dude and spend most of my time now crossing my feet and musing on life's odd little ins and outs. I am quietly engaged in this very pursuit one Saturday morning, warming the plump red velvet pillow that Miss Darcy McGill keeps fluffed and lint-free for me on her dressing table, when who should burst in but the same Miss Darcy McGill. She casts herself upon my bosom and bursts into excessively wet tears as well as enough wails to summon the paramedics.

"Oh, Louie," says she, just plain Louie being my moniker among my intimates. "Oh, Louie, what have I done! What will I do? It is wonderful! It is terrible! My life is ruined. What will happen to Steven if the university regents find out? How can I go back to class? What will I do if he comes here again?" and on and on in like vein, as little dolls—even if they are big dolls—can do when they are sufficiently stimulated.

I am not a man of the world for nothing. I allow her to dampen my whiskers unabated for some time, then look at her wisely. (I may add here that there is no more adept practitioner of the wise look than yours truly, if I do say so myself. My wiseguy look has saved my bacon—and my liver and carp, too—on more than one occasion.) I learned long ago that when a distraught doll throws herself upon your shoulder the wisest thing is to listen and let her talk herself into her own solution.

Some old guy, now deceased, wrote more than somewhat on this theory of mine, and naturally he gets all the credit and the universities teach whole courses based on his writings, which I could have told them about all along, but who am I to quibble at the practice of psychiatry? I think this guy had a beard, like Mr. Abraham Lincoln, but unlike Mr. Abraham Lincoln and myself, he was also burdened with a sheepskin, a nasty smelly old thing were anyone to ask me, which I doubt will ever be the case.

"Oh, Louie," Miss Darcy McGill is sobbing, her long red fingernails clutching rhythmically at my sides, which is a cute habit when I do it, but a little hard on the old hide, if you know what I mean.

I am more than somewhat surprised that this little big doll is wearing these shivs at eight-thirty in the A.M. when she is not scheduled to appear on stage for almost twelve hours yet.

Also, I notice that she still has on the makeup she wears the night before and that it is sadly the worse for wear and is being helped in no way by the waterworks sluicing down her once-piquant features.

So I mull it over and conclude that the dude who visits her in this very dressing room last night must be the cause of these histrionics, though he is a somewhat dignified dude whom one ordinarily would not suspect of churning up a delicate young lady like Miss Darcy McGill into chopped liver.

It strikes me that Mr. Steven Eliot Austen may be something of a bounder. As I take a dim view of anyone breaking the hearts of the little dolls with whom I surround myself, and as Miss Darcy McGill is Queen of Hearts in the Crystal Phoenix Royal Suite Revue, I fear that I myself will have to step in and take action.

But for now, I murmur sweet nothings some auditors of which are pleased to describe as a sort of purr, being that my tone is somewhat rough from the time Butch the Bowser is chasing me down Tropicana Avenue and I dive under a broken board in a parking-lot fence but get a nail in the voice box.

So for now, I soak up the sorrow, and I listen and look wise, which is not an unsuitable appearance to cultivate on any occasion, and you can quote me on that.

♥ Chapter Eight ♥

"A-one-and, two-and, three-and . . . *turn!* And-a-one-and, two-and, three-and . . . *turn!* Turn, chickens! Move! You're not here to lay eggs, darlings! You're here to dance and show off those luscious costumes! From the top."

Sixty stagewise feet stamped and tapped and glided to the ragtime beat of the upright Baldwin. It would have been easier to rehearse to a tape of the show's actual music, but Danny Dove considered himself the spiritual reincarnation of Busby Berkley. Only an emphatic accompanist at the ivory eighty-eights could browbeat a chorus line into a united front, he maintained frequently and loudly.

"Darcy, darling! With your head in the clouds your tiny feetsies don't make crisp little taps on the ground, do they? Concentrate!"

Darcy nodded grimly at the reed-like man uniformed in a black turtleneck, blue jeans, and ostrich-skin cowboy boots. Slight, frenetic Danny Dove was the quintessential choreographer, a terrifying, schizophrenic crossbreed of boot-camp drill sergeant and tooth fairy. She threw herself into the dance steps, counting madly-a-one-and, two-and, three-and . . . *turn!*—until a fellow hoofer hammered past her.

"What's the matter, Darce? Up late?" Trish inquired between smile-locked teeth.

"Right on," Darcy gritted back. "And I borrowed your dress. It'll be dry-cleaned and back by tonight's show."

They glided sideways in different directions, teeth and tap-accoutered toes showing their stuff. Minutes later the

quiet watching, an expression on his face that even Sirene had not yet seen—and Sirene, Darcy recalled with mortification, had seen expressions no person had a right to remember in public.

"I'm not 'little,' " she said, pushing herself upright as Exhibit A.

He stood with her, looking appealingly perplexed, his lips parted as if to say something Darcy might want to hear very badly.

"Darcy," he began, with something impulsive in his tone that equally thrilled and frightened her. "Don't—"

"Hey, got to run! If you're not worried about your next class, I am. 'Bye, Professor."

She spun around and clattered down the far aisle, long brown hair curling like spindrift in her wake. He watched her exit, troubled. The story on her desk remained, the type celebrating Sirene's endlessly long white legs delicately crossed at the ankles.

He swept up the paper-clipped pages and stuck them into the *Norton Anthology of English Literature*. It may not be where Sirene and her escapades belonged, Steven told himself, but he felt safer with her pressed firmly between the closed pages of a book, like a keepsake.

Yet Sirene and Darcy haunted him as he hastened over the tree-shaded campus walks. His mind should have been dwelling on the lyrical ballads of Herbert, Carew, and Lovelace for his class on seventeenth-century poetry, not the exploits of one leggy, twentieth-century chorus girl, and her sibling biographer.

Like Johnson and Boswell, the two seemed—one living a public, flamboyant life, the other chronicling it faithfully.

"Damnation!" Students passing in pairs stared curiously to hear Professor Stevenson Eliot Austen cursing himself under his breath in mid-campus two minutes before the day's last class began.

He noticed them noticing him and tucked his books under his arm, walking on with new briskness, curt nods of recognition, and a grim resolve on his face.

"Who's here again?"

"He is."

"Not the—" Darcy wrenched her chair around to face Midge. "Not—?"

"Not the bedsheet concession! Not the high roller in the broccoli-colored suit. The other one. I even got a look at him as I went by Jake's stand. Not bad."

The other girls paused in removing their wigs.

"The professor?" Jo inquired, her eyes open wider than seemed humanly possible.

"Right."

"I won't see him!" Darcy turned back to the mirror, pulling her hair lock by lock from the bandeau that held it off her face under the various wigs she wore each night.

"Okay." Midge ambled with elaborate unconcern back to her dressing table. "But Jake must consider him a regular already; I heard him telling the professor to go right on down, now that he knew the way."

"Oh . . . expletive deleted!" Darcy's makeup sponge hit her mirror image right in the crimson, lip-glossed kisser. "The least you guys could do is beat it!"

"But we want to *see* him," Trish purred, rising to poise a cocked leg in fishnet hose—an effect distinctly reminiscent of a diamondback rattler to Darcy—on the seat of her chair.

"I've never met a man with a master's degree before."

"A doctor's degree," Darcy corrected glumly.

"A doctor's degree! Oh, that sounds so elevated. I'm not leaving either." Jo planted her barely covered sequined bottom on her dressing table. "He should be along any second anyway."

"All right!" Darcy jumped up, beset by fear and excitement in equal doses. "But just remember not to call me by my first name! I don't want him to confuse me as a student with"—she gestured wildly at the carnival atmosphere—"all this. It would be unlucky," she added forcefully. If there was anything theater people respected around dressing rooms, it was superstition.

"What about Midnight Louie?" Midge was running long nails through the cat's neck ruff as he reclined on Darcy's pillow for the night. "He's as black as a casino bottom line, and that's supposed to be unlucky. He practically lives here."

"Louie never crosses our paths," Jo said dismissively. "He's always following us, looking for a handout, aren't you, boy?" She produced a limp sardine from an opened tin and draped it in front of the cat's extended paws.

They all watched fondly as the animal regarded the offering with the initial regal disdain of cats, then lowered his muzzle and dispatched it with quick efficiency. In that momentary lull, all emergencies forgotten, Professor Stevenson Eliot Austen arrived at their door.

He cleared his throat, not really intending to be heard.

They turned together at the sound, as if choreographed—four tall, feathered, and sequined women, more decorated than dressed—two in black, two in red.

The effect would have overwhelmed a Maurice Chevalier. A mere Austen froze like a hare spotted midmeadow by four silver foxes.

"So this is . . . England," Jo declaimed, her eyes misty enough to melt. She sashayed over to him, rear black satin bows wagging, and twined a rhinestone-ringed arm through his. "I just love knights and armor and chivalry and reading about all that stuff."

"Good for you." Steven glanced down at her possessive hand on his forearm, gently disentangled himself, and gave her hand a consoling pat as he returned it to her.

"Miss . . . McGill?" He looked from one red queen to the other, unable to guess who was who underneath the makeup.

Darcy stepped forward with an apologetic smile. "I guess you're a sensation; we've never had an English professor at our disposal before."

"No indeedy." Irrepressible Trish dashed forward to stand guard on Steven's other side, her hand insinuating itself around his elbow. "Say something in literature," she sighed.

"Ah . . ." Steven capitulated and thrust both hands in his jacket pockets, a gesture that had the advantage of seeming cool, casual, and passive in the face of this barrage of feminine attention.

Darcy felt for him, she really did. She had to give him credit for thrusting himself into the lioness's den this way. And . . . berating herself, she couldn't help observing how attractive he looked with his tailored diffidence sandwiched between such frankly female admirers. Apparently he was beginning to enjoy the juxtaposition too.

"Something . . . literature," he mused, casting his eyes around the dressing room. They landed on the sardine-quenched features of Midnight Louie. "Ah . . . 'The owl and the pussycat went to sea/In a beautiful pea-green boat. They took some honey and plenty of money/Wrapped up in a five-pound note'."

"Oh, that's lovely," Jo enthused.

Steven chuckled modestly.

"I particularly like," Trish murmured against his ear, "the part where they took plenty of money. It must be because the owl was *soooo* wise." Her lips blew playfully in his ear on the endlessly extended "soooo."

"Why would an owl elope with a pussycat, though?" Jo ran her fingers lightly down the lapel of his tweed jacket.

"Well," Steven answered carefully, "we don't know from the text that this was a romantic alliance." He assumed no one present knew the rest of the poem, including the owl's next lines declaring his love.

Trish interrupted him authoritatively. "He went with the pussycat because she was so long and lean and lovely to pet," she articulated, rubbing against him in a routine right out of *Cats!* on Broadway.

"Why don't you wait outside a couple of minutes?" Darcy said sharply. "I'll change and be right out."

Steven smiled and gingerly extracted his arms from their claimants. "Good idea. I'll, uh, see you later. Nice meeting you . . . ladies."

He nodded genially all around and slipped through the ajar door. His head popped back in a moment later. He smiled nervously and pulled it shut behind him.

"Oh, he's *darling!* I adore shy men." Trish threw herself into her chair again before looking severely at Darcy. "But you can't have my red dress again."

"Thanks," Darcy said sardonically, jerking open her locker. Her own "emergency-date" dress hung there now, a soft column of magenta silk. Below poised two bronze-leather high-heeled sandals.

"You shouldn't have teased him like that." She tore off her heavily beaded costume and hung it on its proper pegs.

The others were busy doing the same.

"Most of the guys we see are always coming on so strong," Jo said. "It's kinda nice to see a man you have to work on."

"I know," Darcy said under her breath, cursing the back zipper that had stuck in the delicate silk right between her shoulderblades.

"Here, let me." Midge came over to untangle the snarl. Her hands were motherly as she patted the dress into place on Darcy's shoulders. "They didn't mean to aggravate anyone, Darce. The professor's such a welcome change of pace for us. Why do you suppose he keeps showing up like this? Can't he just call and ask for a date?"

"It's not a date!" Darcy burst out.

Midge's brown eyes were as dubious as a bridle-shy mare's.

"We have things to talk about, that's all."

"It's not a date," Jo mimicked impishly. "Look at the girl in that new dress! I'd hate to see what you wear on a *real* date."

"Oh . . . just keep quiet." Darcy hurled herself into her chair to begin pinning up her hair in a configuration that would match last week's style. "It's not what you think. You just don't understand!" Her fingers shook, stabbing the pins into her scalp. *Now what?* her excited, anxious mind wondered. Why was he here, and how long could she keep up the persona of Sirene now that she was caught between two worlds? Did she even want to?

"Good luck, kid." Jo's hand on her shoulder interrupted Darcy's inner rush to utter panic.

"Yeah," Trish seconded. "Whatever's up, have a good time. Or a bad time, if that's what you want. Only find out what kind of cologne he wears. I know two hundred thousand crap players who could use a little finesse."

"Take care," Midge wished her softly from the silent side of the room.

Darcy took a deep breath. In the many mirrors that fractured the costume-crammed space into a dozen, glitter-dusted pieces, Sirene gazed back at her. Her crimson fingernails shone jewel-bright against the interesting clash of the magenta dress. She looked gorgeous and exotic and utterly unlike Darcy.

Of course Steven Austen believed in Sirene; Darcy herself, her writing, and, now, acting talent had forced him to.

If only Darcy herself could believe in Sirene now, she told herself, wishing her stomach weren't kicking up a chorus line storm under the clinging dress. If only her heart weren't pounding like Max on the old Baldwin upright at the undreamed idea of being in his arms again even as she hated the thought of tricking him once more. If only she weren't beginning to wonder to whom her heart belonged— to daytime Darcy she knew so well, to bold post-midnight Sirene who surprised the hell out of her. Or to Stevenson Eliot Austen.

She ducked out the door with a final "Goodnight" to the gang.

He was pushing off the slightly soiled wall he'd been leaning against, his hands safely in his pockets, as if he thought she planned to encumber him.

She didn't move or speak, but stood in little-girl recital position—feet neatly together, hands crossed on her small bronze purse held before her. She even forgot that a demure posture could hardly mask the predatory glamour of Sirene.

"I wanted to talk to you again," Steven said slowly, coming toward her.

"About my sister, Darcy?"

He paused, in speech and motion. Then he removed his glasses so that she could see right into the bottomless silver-gray well of them.

"About . . . you, Sirene."

Darcy felt shock stiffen her shoulders.

"If we could go somewhere private . . ." He smiled. "I know, there's no place 'private' in Vegas. I was thinking of someplace outside Vegas. My house, on the desert. I think you'd like seeing it. If you can stay up that late."

She shrugged and walked over to him, not trusting herself to speak, walked with him down the long empty corridors to the stairs. Late leavers raced past them now and again, pounding exuberantly down the echoing concrete tunnel, their still-madeup faces contrasting oddly with casual street clothes, so Steven and Sirene seemed to be caught in a shower of meteoric mimes.

"You're sure it's not too late?" he asked in that deep, thoughtful voice that had first sent shivers down her spine in class.

"No," she said. "We all need to stay up a couple hours after a show, to let the adrenaline ebb."

But it *was* too late, Darcy thought, knowing that tears shouldn't be stinging Sirene's false-lash-framed eyes, that her painted talons should be digging into Steven's arm instead of keeping to themselves.

Darn that pushy glamourpuss, Sirene! Darcy thought, already spinning plots that would dramatically inter Sirene forever. Maybe a car wreck in the desert. Or a . . . Mob hit. Perhaps a mysterious disappearance. *That darn Sirene.* She'd done it. Sirene had all too successfully seduced Darcy's dream lover, and she hadn't even had to exist to do it.

♥ Chapter Nine ♥

The desert at night shifted in fluid ripples all the way to the horizon where it beached itself on an endless, ink-black strand of sky. Ribbons of road undulated over the drifts, caught only for short spaces in the artificial roving moonlight of the headlights. It wasn't hard to drive into the heart of the desert from Las Vegas; the city straddled the Interstate atop dessicated sands that only soaked up four blessed inches of rainfall a year.

The prow of Steven's silver sedan ploughed furrows into the opaque night scenery. Darcy, in the passenger seat, twisted back once to view Las Vegas shrinking in the rear window frame, its carnival blare of lights fading to a fairyland twinkle.

"You miss the bright lights already?" Steven asked without looking away from the road unraveling in his headlight beams.

Darcy squirmed around to face forward again, forgetting that she was Sirene and that the rasp of shifting silk would draw his eyes. She propped her feet against the floorboard and made a momentary bridge of her body while jerking her skirt down to a decorous position.

The car offered plenty of legroom, at least. Darcy eased back into the cushions, grateful to be off her dance-worn feet.

"No, I don't miss it," she finally answered. "I just never saw it from here at night. Is your house far?"

"Not very."

The dashboard lit his profile, casting angular shadows where she hadn't seen them before. He wore his glasses for driving, of course, and reminded her momentarily of Indiana Jones before he traded in his professorial props for a fedora and a bullwhip. The idea that Stevenson Eliot Austen also harbored a second secretly swashbuckling personality made her smile.

"What's so amusing?"

"Nothing. Only I didn't expect you to drive a Honda Accord."

"You surely didn't expect a Ferrari?"

"No . . ."

"It's the only car that will run uphill with the air conditioning on full without losing power." His dashboard-lit profile jerked in the direction of the shadowy hunched shoulders of the desert-ringing mountains. "It's perfect for this climate and location."

"Do you always choose things for such practical reasons?"

"Usually." He looked in her direction again, curious. "You seem pensive."

Darcy figuratively kicked herself. Of course she seemed different! She'd been sitting here like a normal woman, relaxing in the presence of a man she knew, admired, and liked more than a little. She'd forgotten that the indefatigable Sirene was always "on."

"What's 'pensive' mean?" she asked perkily, sitting to attention with an inciting squirm of silk.

"Melancholy, out of humor. You know where the idea of 'humors' originates, don't you? Medieval philosophers thought that the body had four internal states that expressed themselves in four personality types. The melancholy humor was just one. Alexander Pope wrote 'Il Penseroso,' a long poem about it. 'Penseroso' is Italian. 'Penseroso'. . . pensive, see?"

A silence pervaded the car.

"No." Darcy shifted again, this time hoisting her skirt a few intriguing inches. "Can't you put it in words of one syllable?"

" 'Pensive' means sad," he said shortly.

"Oh. No, I'm not sad, just tired from kicking my can all over the Crystal Phoenix stage tonight." She leaned her head back and inhaled deeply. "I love it when the air-conditioning's not on; I think I can smell the sagebrush."

His teeth flashed pirate-white in the dim car, but his glasses winked only a white reflection, like a lighthouse signal, as he glanced her way again.

"Quite a romantic, aren't you?"

"Aren't *you?*"

His hands moved to grip the steering wheel, as if reminded of a need for control. "Not usually," he said with a certain grimness Darcy longed to explore. Sirene, of course, simply exploited it.

"Now *you* sound pensive, Doc." She wriggled over on the softly upholstered seat to bridge the gap created by the bucket seats. "Is that why you wanted to see me? To cheer you up?"

"No. Sirene—" Impatience throbbed in his voice, then stilled as he turned to look at her. She'd arranged her face so it tilted, almost resting, against the shoulder seam of his jacket. "Not . . . not while I'm driving."

She writhed her way back, leaving the light farewell tracks of her nails on his sleeve. "I've got to get close sometime," she warned. "I have an assignment."

"Oh? What kind of 'assignment?' "

"From Trish. The other red queen, remember?"

"How could I forget?" he murmured prayerfully to the dome light.

"Anyway, she told me she loved your—"

The car aimed toward the gravel shoulder, then straightened abruptly. "My . . . what?" he asked cautiously.

"Your shaving lotion. Or cologne. I'm not supposed to come back without knowing the brand."

"Are you chorus girls always so silly?"

Sirene considered it. "No. Only on nights and weekends."

His laughter rang against the closed car windows, sounding amplified and private at the same time.

"I'd rather know your pipe tobacco brand," she confessed next.

"My pipe tobacco! Sirene, I rarely smoke, and never on campus."

"Your clothes reek of it, sweetie." A bold hand slipped inside his jacket pocket. "But who's complaining? It's a heckuva lot better than mothballs."

Her fanned fingers, fresh from aromatic explorations of his pocket, wafted under his nose. The car swerved as he caught her hand and restored it to her lap on her side of the car.

"You're like your sister," he noted.

"Oh, really?" Sirene sounded mildly dubious, but Darcy's heart inside her pounded into panic. Had he guessed? "How?"

"Always poking your nose into other people's business, as she does in those stories about you. Don't they bother you?"

"She has to write about something, and I'm handy. Nope, I guess it doesn't upset me. I mean, if she were making stuff up about me, it'd be different. But everything she writes is the truth."

Steven winced as he spun the wheel. Ahead of them, the

106

headlights scythed a wide path of light, revealing a curving private driveway between tall hedges of oleander. In a few moments Steven swung the car into a driveway, punched out the lights, and turned off the ignition.

"Home, sweet home," he announced as he got out of the car.

For once, Sirene was speechless.

"Watch out for snakes," he warned, opening her car door. They glanced down together. The dome light illuminated long white legs emerging from a crumpled swatch of magenta silk skirt and a patch of gray-gravel driveway planted with impossibly high-heeled bronze sandals on arched insteps. "On the other hand, I don't think they could reach that high."

"Snakes? What kind?"

"Mojave, sidewinder, and speckled rattlers. But don't worry; there are no diamondbacks or garter snakes. You don't wander far from the city lights much, do you?"

She shuddered. "No, thank goodness."

His hand levered her out of the seat; she was almost in his arms before her equilibrium returned. Interweaving scents of vintage pipe tobacco and fresh cologne mingled headily. She'd never noticed the cologne before. Had he used it for *her* . . . or Sirene, rather?

"It's quiet out here," she said. "Doesn't it give you the willies?" Darkness and stillness seemed two of a kind exerting their mingled spell all around them; cold made a crowd, edging its chill early morning message into every pore.

"Quite the contrary." His hand on her elbow lightly guided her up the single step to the front door. "It gives me solitude."

From the wild array of cacti and rangy shrubs in the

front yard, Steven's place resembled a typical desert residence—low, long, and cowering under the stingy shade of whatever greenery could be induced to grow near the house.

Darcy was relieved to hear her heels echo on entry-hall quarry tile as they moved inside and she clicked back into snake-free territory and the comforts of civilization. Steven's turn of a switch made several lamps scattered throughout the main room explode into cheery light at once. She got an overall impression of wood and warmth.

"Why did you bring me here?"

He stood in the shadowy part of the room, near the dark umbilical passage of entryway. "You don't know, and you still came? Why?"

"I don't know." She let her purse dangle idly, twisting it against her leg by its golden strap. "I thought you did."

"Listen, Sirene, I do want to talk to you, seriously. About, ah, last week."

"All of last week? Or a specific day?"

"About . . . Friday. Night." Steven patted his pockets automatically and somewhat absentmindedly, then looked to the mantel across the room. Every word seemed to screw him deeper into conversational hardwood. He ambled over to dislodge a pipe from its rack and turned back to her with a disarming smile. "You know what I mean."

"No. I don't know."

Sirene dropped her dainty gilt purse on the cushy brown leather Chesterfield sofa that fronted the fireplace. A folded plaid wool blanket lay over the top, trailing fringe. Smoke-aged knotty pine, buffed to a Golden Retriever sheen, paneled the room's walls.

"All these yours, Doc?" Sirene's bedaggered nails walked over the ridges of books lining the shelves of built-in knotty-pine cases.

"My name's Steven. And yes, except for the ones that are borrowed."

He sounded distracted. Darcy figured it was Sirene's loose-hipped stroll along the bookcases. When she turned, he was still patting his fingers across the manteltop and looking nowhere but there.

"Here." She ankled back to her purse, bent, pulled out a gilt-embossed book of Crystal Phoenix matches, and walked over to him. "Here's the kind of book you need now."

As she struck, the match instantly flared into strong flame; Van and Nicky believed in quality down to the last detail. She inhaled the perfume of fresh-struck sulphur.

He stared over its dancing diamond of light into her eyes. She could see the match flame—and herself—reflected in perfect miniature in his lenses.

Reaching for her hand, he guided it to the pipe bowl, then inhaled with curt intensity to stoke the dormant to-bacco. There was something covertly sexual about their mute cooperation, something that would have been a big hit in a 1940s *film noir,* she thought. Darcy stood as if hypno-tized, letting him hold her hand to the pipe even as the matchflame licked at her highly flammable false nails, even as the heat intensified on her fingertips.

The tobacco took, and he jerked the bowl away, moving the pipe from his lips and bringing her hand closer to blow the flame fiercely against her for a microsecond before it winked out.

"No harm done?" he asked. He puffed on the pipe; a scent like cinnamon-sprinkled vanilla swaddled her head.

"No." She tossed the matchbook to the mantel. "What *about* Friday? Night."

"I wanted to explain."

"Explain what?"

"That it won't happen again."

Sirene's hands fisted pugnaciously on her hips before Darcy could restrain them. "You brought me all the way out here to tell me that you *don't* want to sleep with me?"

"No. It's not a matter of 'want,' it's a matter of 'shouldn't.' I didn't mean to, the last time . . . or rather, er, the first time, which will *be* the last time—"

Sirene's weight cocked to one hip as her mouth soured at the reference. "You do a mean 'didn't mean to,' Doc."

"It was a mistake."

"I'll say!"

Sirene turned to stare down at the hearth-stacked logs. Like herself, they needed only a match to set them off. What on earth did the man want now? Darcy wondered, sharing some of her doppelganger's spontaneous ire. He apparently planned to renounce her body. What was he after—her soul?

The lightest of touches, tentative as a cobweb, stirred the silk on her shoulder. She turned, her eyes as ablaze as her dress. "Do you mean to say that you brought me out here on false pretenses, Professor?"

He looked as if a sidewinder had slipped in with them and he'd just noticed it.

"Now, see here! I'm merely taking an interest in your honor, since you seem loath to do it yourself. You should be flattered."

" 'Flattered'?" The lurid blue shadow on Sirene's eyelids flashed like summer lightning.

"Flattered that I'm interested in something, ah, other than"—the hand holding the pipe made a diffident gesture indicating the length of Sirene's silk-sheened torso—"than your more obvious attractions."

"Like what?"

"Less material aspects, like—"

If he said "soul," Darcy was going to let Sirene belt him one.

"Like . . . your mind," Steven finished in high moral certitude.

"So what's wrong with it?"

"It's, er, primitive. Charming," he hastened to answer the growing glint in her eye. "But primitive."

"You thought primitive was plenty okey-dokey last Friday. Night." She repeated even the long hesitation between Friday and night that he endowed on references to their previous encounter.

"Sirene, you must understand." He paced, ignoring the pipe but cradling it in one palm like a worry stone. He turned back to her dramatically. "I was out of my mind last Friday night!"

"Gee, thanks. You mean you're one of those Heckyl-and-Jeckyl guys? All hot to trot one day and ice a la carte the next?"

Steven paused by the mantel, setting his smouldering pipe back in its rack. "You mean Heckyl and Hyde," he repeated mechanically. "I mean, *Jekyll* and Hyde! You confuse the Dickens out of me, Sirene, but I assure you I'm no split personality. The man I'm named after, Robert Louis Stevenson, wrote the book on it, for heaven's sake!"

Sirene frowned prettily. "Robert Louis Stevenson? Isn't he a middleweight? Goes by 'Lightning Robbie Louis'?"

"No!" Steven neared her abruptly, then calmed to let his hands settle persuasively on her shoulders. "Look here, Sirene, you can't go through life on a purely material level."

"It's worked so far. What's the problem, Professor? Haven't you ever had any girlfriends?"

He hastened to correct that hasty impression. "I've had

111

mature relationships, but nothing like, nothing like—"

"Friday. Night." Her lips had tightened in a half-mocking smile. She saw his eyelashes flutter as his gaze focused on her mouth, then jerked away.

"No," he agreed. "I lost my head. I've never met anyone like you. Sirene?"

"Hmmm?" The weight of his hands was driving the silk sideways on one shoulder. She felt his hand warm more and more of her skin before he did. The pinpointed sensation was so seductive, she swayed toward him. His hands tightened, only intensifying their effect.

"Sirene." He was whispering now, and why shouldn't he speak softly? Their lips were on the same level and drawing closer. "About the men Darcy writes about. You don't . . . with all of them, with . . . many of them . . . you know—"

"Friday. Night?"

"That's right. Darcy's just exaggerating. You're not really—"

"Not really what?"

Now the ebbing magenta silk had caught his wandering eyes. Fascinated, he watched while Darcy felt the fabric's slow, inevitable slide drape halfway down her arm. Steven's forefinger tapped nervously on her bare skin, then found the groove between the bones at the very top of her shoulder, the one into which his finger fit as if into a glove. The tap evolved into a rhythmic, unconscious stroking.

"No," he said, his expression as disoriented as his words. "You're not . . . I'm not . . ."

A dull matchlike burn ignited deep in Darcy's body. The furnace of her heart pumped in four-four time, as if in thrall to a rhythm far more demanding than any Danny Dove could cajole from the upright Baldwin. Steven's stroking finger made itself at home in the small subtle notch of her

"That's not what I want off," he said firmly. He pounced, dragging her back down to the air-cushioned leather, which responded to his intentions much as Sirene did—with frequent, nearly inaudible sighs.

A flag of surrender in the form of a shapeless length of magenta silk soon waved over the sofa back on Steven's elevated hand. He dropped it overboard with stylish disdain and returned to the main event transpiring on the sofa's stormy surface.

"I'm cold now," Sirene complained, laughing.

"I thought the fire was making you hot."

"I said I was feeling overheated. I didn't blame anything in particular."

Silence prevailed, then Steven rose over the sofa back, stretching out one arm until his fingers pinched a fold of blanket and he hoisted it over the couch.

In a moment Sirene was snuggling into the sandwiching warmth of a wool blanket and a wooly male body.

"You're incorrigible," he complained, sucking in his breath.

"Another big word again," she countercharged. "Tell me what it means," she demanded fondly.

"It means. . . ." He looked down at her, squinting. "It means you look even more terrific in soft focus; I hope the eyeglass industry never finds out about you. They'd name you a public hazard."

"That's what 'incorrigible' means?" Sirene batted her heavy-duty eyelashes.

"No, incorrigible means. . . ." Steven stared at her again, trying to define the indefinable. "It means . . . teasing, maddening, inciting to riot, impossibly addictive, a triumph of matter over mind."

"I'm all that?"

"And more. Let me count the ways."

"Stev-en!" she shrieked as the blanket heaved between them.

"I can only count with my fingers," he apologized soberly. "We written word guys are lousy at math."

"Steven." She rolled atop him suddenly. "I love it when you're playful, but I—don't you want to, to . . . ?"

"Friday . . . night?"

They laughed together, but Sirene was the first to stop. "You could undress me till Doomsday, Professor, but unless you do something after that you're still missing the boat."

His gray eyes darkened to charcoal. Sirene could see the red flare of flames dancing on the fireplace-side of his irises. She could see her indelibly painted face looking back hopefully at her.

A lithesome shadow flitted across his expression.

"If only I could believe that we two have something . . . special. We're so ill-matched."

She shut her eyes. Steven saw the artificial black lashline at the root of her lids; it only made her look oddly vulnerable to him, as if pieces of her more precious than mere decoration could break off in his hands as easily as the glued-on artifices she hid behind.

"Sirene," he began, sensing for the first time some emotional depth in her that both stirred and frightened him.

Her eyes opened. In the dancing firelight they seemed to sparkle like Darcy's did in sunlight. They looked strangely hazel-blue to his unaided eyesight, strangely blurred. Then she spoke through the tears that thickened her voice even as they sheened her eyes.

"Steven," she said, sounding more serious than he had ever heard Sirene speak. "You've touched my heart and mind more than anyone . . . ever. Don't be afraid to touch me."

Darcy—not Sirene—stared hopefully into his eyes. She'd pushed the charade as far as she could go alone. If he didn't hear her love speaking through every sense and in every way but plain words, it was over. She had never wanted to take a prisoner, just to win the war of longing. She didn't want to have to seduce him forever.

She fell asleep in the aftermath of his arms. She fell asleep because it was five o'clock in the morning and way past even her early-morning bedtime, because she was tired, and because she was happy.

Morning came later, much later, when she finally unglued her lashes at a tickle of daylight too overpowering to ignore any longer. She faced into the unreadably near red neon of a digital alarm clock. Darcy backed off and squinted. The big hand was on twelve and the little hand on ten.

"I guess that'll prove I went to school. A genuine ten o'clock scholar," she giggled to herself, sitting up, the plaid blanket cocooned around her. Her feet touched icy tiled floor and retracted.

"Good morning."

Steven stood in the doorway—no, he filled it like a revelation. He was wearing khaki pants and a sweater the color of mist-gray purple heather seen in soft focus on postcards of Scotland. He also wore a slightly askew smile that was one part shyness and three parts sex appeal that stripped the awkward morning-after of all its pretensions.

"Some Friday night," Darcy said, rubbing her eyes. "Did I miss anything good?"

His smile grew wicked with memory. "Not too much."

"You, uh, dragged me in here?"

He nodded.

Darcy whistled softly. "I'm impressed. I'm a big girl. You should see Danny Dove trying to demonstrate a lift with me. Hernia city."

"You're lighter than you look."

"And you're stronger," she said admiringly.

His eyes dropped. "Must come from grading papers. I put your, ah, things in the bathroom. I thought you'd want a shower before breakfast."

"Sure thing." She sprang out of bed, expertly flipping the blanket over her shoulder Indian-princess style. "I'm still a little stiff."

They regarded each other, not sure whether to retreat into unspoken embarrassment or advance into shared bawdy reminiscence.

"I won't comment on that," he volunteered. "Come to the kitchen when you're ready."

"Right," Darcy said, grinning insouciantly.

She bounced into the adjacent bathroom as soon as he had left. Her clothes, such as they were, hung from a behind-the-door hook. It was a no-nonsense bathroom with white fixtures all in a row, marine-blue tile, and a split shower curtain with a plentitude of penguins marching across a transparent plastic background.

She sang in the shower, wondering how she would look in designer penguin if Steven happened to peek in. But he didn't, and in some ways she was just as glad.

At least she'd finally accomplished her assignment for Trish, Darcy thought, replacing the oval of brown soap in its built-in ceramic dish. Newport, she cataloged the custom brand, a racy nineteenth-century men's scent from Caswell-Massey in New York. She ought to have known that Stevenson Eliot Austen would succumb to no over-the-counter olfactory blandishments.

She liked the bathroom; there wasn't anything extraneous in it. Darcy leaned into her image in the chrome-framed medicine-cabinet mirror. She wished she could wash off the old makeup but didn't dare. It was too soon to strip off her mask. She leaned so close her lashes almost buffed the mirror.

"Steven," she said forthrightly, "I love your house!" She leaned nearer yet, so she could hardly focus on herself. Her voice lowered. "I love you!"

Her hands clapped over her mouth. Her eyes widened to Carol Channing dimensions. She was alone with the shower steam and her vocalized thoughts. Steven was far too . . . intuitive . . . to invade her privacy.

She lifted a smaller, sink-size bar of Newport to her face. "I love you," she whispered to it with a kiss. The scent flooding her nostrils made her almost giddy. She spun in the small room, her bare feet feeling every groove in the tiled floor, and spiraled herself into a roll of penguinized Saran-wrap.

"I love you," she whispered, wrapped in her own arms and the shower curtain. Unrolling with a dancer's fluid skill, she snatched up a towel and rubbed her cheek on its reassuring terry-cloth stubble. "I do. Honest I do."

Back at the mirror Darcy dampened her flying tendrils and pushed them back into the smooth off-the-face order that Sirene favored. No more disorder in the dress or Cavalier poetry for Sirene now that morning had come. Her stomach growled unexpectedly. Good lord, but she was hungry! She sure hoped Steven could cook too.

The odor of bacon being done to death crushed her optimism. Wrapping a large blue bath towel around her, she rummaged in the bedroom bureau until she found some wooly socks to pull on and hotfooted it for the kitchen.

Steven squinted owlishly at the black iron frypan that smoked on the stove from a distance, with bemused reproach.

Darcy grabbed a hotpad, pinched it over the frying pan handle, and escorted it hastily to the back stoop.

"I got carried away," he said behind her. "I thought a hearty breakfast of eggs and bacon after, after . . ." His thoughts became censorable and died as quick a death as the bacon.

Outside, the desert morning was brewing up a sun-steeped rose-gold glow of dawn. Far away, the mountains hovered smoky blue on the horizon.

"It's all right, Doc," Darcy said briskly, returning the cooled pan to the stove. "I'll drain and chop this stuff into an omelet. It'll be just like Bac-Os."

"OK." Steven seemed glad enough to surrender the breakfast project to her. What he did not seem ready to abandon was a certain anxiety about her appearance.

"Sirene . . . are you sure that thing won't . . . come off?"

"Not if I keep tucking it in tighter, like this," she said blithely, demonstrating with a savage jerk that rewrapped the terry cloth under her arm.

He glanced to her feet.

"I found them in a drawer of unmatched socks." She wriggled her toes in the oversized stocking feet while draining grease into the kitchen sink. "What's wrong? Do they match?"

He donned his glasses to check it out. "I can't tell. I don't suppose it matters, but you do rather resemble a teenage bag lady."

"That's very good. An apt description, Professor. But your floors are cold, and I don't want to totter around on my instep-grinders. Besides,"—she sidled up against him while returning with two handfuls of eggs from the refrigerator—"I thought we were friends now and didn't have to be so formal."

His hands wrapped her bare upper arms as gingerly as she cradled the uncooked breakfast eggs.

"Of course we're friends," he answered, "but maybe you'd better concentrate on cooking."

Soon their forks were dissecting a fluffy blond omelet laced with peppers, cheese, onions, and black bacon bits.

"What d'you usually eat for breakfast?" Darcy asked sunnily, drinking her grapefruit juice.

"Cereal and milk," he answered sheepishly. "It's fast."

"So are you, baby," Sirene interjected with a wink.

"Er, Sirene," he began, his fork exiling bacon and peppers into color-keyed groups upon his plate.

"Yes?" She peered pertly over her steaming cup of black coffee, knowing he wasn't used to staring at bare-shouldered ladies across his tiny breakfast table.

Steven put down his implements and met her gaze.

"We haven't discussed some things. Like whether you're protected—"

"Sure I am," Sirene interjected lightly. "The Crystal Phoenix has got a top security force."

"Not *that*," he said. "You know what I mean. Are you protected from—us?"

"Heavens, yes, Steven. Don't look so guilty. I know how to take care of myself. I'm on the pill."

"Oh." He looked more disappointed than relieved. "I suppose it's, it's the fact that you . . . that you lead a somewhat liberated lifestyle."

"No." She put down her own fork and met his eyes with her own. "It's the opposite. It's the fact that I'm a dancer. Dancers can't afford physical irregularities in our schedule or monthly sicknesses. Old Man Rhythm don't look kindly on natural ups and downs. It's 'tote that fan, lift that leg. Dance with pain, or there's no gain.' So, a lot of us take the pill as a matter of routine." She smiled. "But it's nice of you to ask."

"Good God, why shouldn't I ask? I should have thought of it much sooner. I come charging into your life and somehow keep ending up in bed with you. Instead of unraveling Darcy's mind as I meant to do, I keep undressing you, as I certainly never intended—"

"Oh." Sirene pouted thoughtfully as she sipped the hot coffee. "Do you want to dress me this morning?" she inquired throatily. "Would that make you feel better, poor man?"

He glowered over his glass frames. "Probably, but not in the way I meant. You must start taking these things—your personal liaisons seriously, Sirene."

"Why?"

"Because 'life is earnest; life is real!' You must live it with discipline and order."

"That doesn't sound like anything those Cavalier guys would say. Were they a football team, or what?"

"What?" he croaked.

"I thought they might have been one of the new franchises. You know, the Cincinnati Cavaliers or something. I don't pay much attention to sports."

"They've been dead for over three hundred years!"

Sirene shrugged knowingly. "The way some of the teams have been playing lately, they could've been dead at least that long. You should hear Nostradamus moan about the bath he's taking on the football odds."

"Nostradamus. Cavaliers. Football. Bookies. Odds." Steven pushed away his plate. "Sirene, you soon will have me living in two worlds and thoroughly lost. You're driving me to distraction."

"I'll tell you what," she returned seriously, chewing her toast. "Why don't I go put my clothes on; that ought to help your distraction."

She rose, swept their empty plates to sinkside, and paused in the doorway to the living room.

"You know what I think is bothering you, Doc?" she asked over a shoulder that seemed more naked than bare. "I think it's too much 'li-qui-fac-tion.'" Her torso twitched effectively beneath the boxy roll of towel that wrapped it. "Those big words'll lead you into a life of crime every time."

Steven leaned back in the light kitchen chair and absently reached for his untouched coffee. An absent-minded sip seared his mouth and sprayed into the quick intervention of his napkin.

Everything around him, he mused glumly, was becoming, like Sirene, too damn hot to handle.

But she was subdued and decorous when she reappeared, even if her dress still sizzled with late-night sheen and supple motion. He glanced at the delicate shoes.

"My first class is at one, so I've got to get into town. But if you think your footwear can handle it, there's something —someone—I'd like to show you out back."

"Sure," Sirene agreed. "I'd love to eyeball any skeletons you keep in your closet, Doc."

"This is hardly a skeleton," he remarked as he led her to the back of the lot. Bushes and trees ringed the yard, giving the illusion of domesticated greenery. Beyond this tightknit oasis the sere desert landscape unrolled with only the intermittent profile of a tall Joshua tree yucca offering any shade higher than a creosote or sagebrush bush might provide for a pocket gopher.

Under a small circle of cultivated trees stood a small shed. They paused in the shade by a split-rail fence as Steven put his fingers to his lips and whistled.

Swaying out from the thick shade came the sure-footed form of a rangy dapple-gray horse.

"Oh, I love him! Her! It!" Darcy dropped Sirene's usual blasé tones. "A horse! Steven, no wonder you love it here."

"I never said that I did," he said curiously.

"Oh, but you do; you can't hide it. I didn't know you rode."

"I'm not a master of equitation, but I enjoy the informal ramble."

"Equitation! Steven, there's a big word even for riding a horse? What's his name?"

"Your instincts are right," he observed as the horse's questing muzzle dipped into her outstretched hand. Clumsy velvet lips nibbled her skin. "He's an Appaloosa stallion. I call him Quaker because he likes his oats. And he *is* gray." He studied her shining face. "Maybe you'd like to come out and ride him sometime."

"Oh, yes. Only—"

Steven's eyebrows raised quizzically.

Darcy curled her fingernails into her palm and stroked the horse's pinkish muzzle with her less-lethal knuckles. She answered Steven's mute question with a rush of words.

"Only . . . dancing and horseback riding don't mix. You use different muscles, and doing one will ruin you for the other."

"I see."

Darcy could see him withdrawing from her forever behind his patches and his pipes. Steven was hunting common ground, some mutual interest to explain or excuse their uncommon physical alliance. And she couldn't even offer him the sop of Sirene's horse craziness because horseback riding was incompatible with her dancing. It occurred to Darcy that a lot of things had always been incompatible with her dancing.

"No, you don't see," she burst out. "I love him! I'd love to visit him here. Maybe a sedate walk around the yard. Oh, I don't know. Maybe all that about dancing and riding not mixing are old wives' tales."

"I didn't mean to upset you." Steven smiled and put his arms around her. The sweater's fuzzy, foggy texture felt wonderful. Sirene pushed Darcy boldly into his embrace while Quaker nickered. Was it dismay at his sudden conversion from centerpiece to equine background?

"You don't fool me, Sirene." Steven's voice was strangely tender. "I've seen through your act."

Darcy froze in the dear, fuzzy circle of his arms. "You have?"

"It took me a while to figure it out," he added with charming sternness. "But it suddenly came up like thunder out of China 'cross the bay. I sense some fey aspect of Darcy glimmering in you."

Her hands clutched the tenuous carapace of his sweater as her breath caught in her throat.

"At first, I could only glimpse it now and again. And that's when I realized that all that flash was only an act."

"And you're not angry with me?" she asked cautiously.

He chuckled into her ear. "How could I be angry with you for merely being human? Heaven knows I'm only too human."

His fingers tightened on her ribs and Darcy began calculating shamelessly how late he could be for his first class.

"I know it's been a lonely, hard life you've had, in its way."

"No, Steven, I—"

"Now don't interrupt." His fingertip tapped the tip of her upturned nose. A faraway light illuminated the satin-gray eyes, as it did in class when he read from his favorite selections. "I can see that despite the surface glamour of your profession, it calls for tremendous dedication and single-mindedness.

"You are an athlete, an artist," he intoned, embracing his subject as totally as he had her. "You cannot be expected to lead a normal life or to attack life in quite the normal way. I understand," Steven finished. "Beneath the rhinestones and the feathers lurks a sensitive soul, every bit the match of Darcy's. I should never have worried about her. I see why you fascinate her; you fascinate me. I'm obviously very . . . fond of you, Sirene. I expect you to be nothing more than what you are; that's good enough for me."

He sealed his promise by leaning closer and kissing her lips with leisurely surety. "Well?" he demanded, so delighted with his new broad-mindedness he never noticed her shock.

"I'm, I'm speechless."

"Oh." He seemed momentarily disappointed. "Then perhaps, while you're regaining your voice—" He pulled her deeper into his arms for another longer, more consuming kiss.

Sirene responded wholeheartedly, dragging a confused Darcy with her.

It was wonderful, as Darcy had sobbed into the stoic presence of Midnight Louie the week before. She'd never dreamed she'd be wrapped in a lip lock with Professor Stevenson Eliot Austen under a spreading olive tree and the benign liquid-brown gaze of an Appaloosa stud.

Rare desert scents drifted delicately past them on the frayed ends of a soft scarf of wind. Sun dappled through the shade, falling like golden coins. God was in his heaven and all was right with the world, although Sirene would never understand that the expression came from Browning, which she probably thought was a town in Montana.

"You know," Steven said excitedly, "the best way to break it to Darcy might be for the three of us to get together to discuss her stories. That's it. We're all interested in her work, aren't we? Later, perhaps we can tell her the rest. What do you think?"

"It sounds all right," she answered, her mind pedaling madly. He hadn't seen through her at all; he just had decided that Sirene was more complex than she seemed. Damn Sirene—she was simple as two-to-one odds!

"It sounds perfect," Steven happily contradicted her. "But for now, delicious girl, I'd better get you back to your apartment and me back to campus for my date with thirty-some literal-minded literature students."

The casual weight of his arm across her shoulders as he guided her back to the house was everything Darcy had ever hoped for from Steven, not only ecstasy by night but tender camaraderie by day. This scenario couldn't have had a happier ending than if she had written every word herself, she mused in numb despair. The only problem was, she'd written two heroines into the script.

Steven's hand was patting her arm in an avuncular fashion that still managed to send her stomach into a nosedive.

"It'll be splendid to have the three of us get together," he crowed, a man basking in the resolution of a troubling dilemma. "We can be open about our relationship; I can exempt myself from critiquing Darcy's little fictions about you; perhaps she'll stop altogether once she sees that you and I are . . . well, more than bare acquaintances." Steven rubbed his hands together in anticipation. "I can hardly wait to see you and Darcy, side by side."

♥ Chapter Eleven ♥

Professor Stevenson Eliot Austen sat on the edge of his desk, his glass frames open on some papers beside him, a book propped on his khaki-covered knee, his finger needlessly marking the place while he recited a favorite prose passage from memory.

Spellbound, the class heard him out with unusually respectful attention.

From her customary seat at the very back of the room, Darcy studied him. Steven had favored Sirene with a lingering farewell kiss in the car when they'd parted a few hours before, outside her apartment. Now, his eyes seemed satisfied to overlook Darcy among the student faces so raptly fixed on his.

The dishwater blonde theater major in front of Darcy leaned across to her girlfriend and raised an eyebrow. "Dishy," she stage-whispered in newfound appreciation, still keeping both eyes on Steven's professorial performance.

Of course he would seem more attractive, Darcy thought with metaphorically gritted teeth. He was a man falling in love. For the first time in anyone's memory he'd worn a casual sweater and slacks to class, shedding his former stiffness of manner along with his more mannered clothing.

Steven was newly expansive, charming, confident—everything no one else had seen in the English professor until Darcy had dreamed up Sirene and liberated this, this . . . monster . . . of her own making.

Darcy doodled in her journal, oblivious to the resonant voice that had once transfixed only her. Men! They were all alike, she thought self-righteously, hating herself for descending into rank clichés that she would have ruthlessly expunged from a page. Show them a makeup-frosted face and a seminude body and they would all crumble like chocolate-chip cookies. Even Professor Stevenson Eliot Austen. Especially Professor Stevenson Eliot Austen.

Her pencil tip pressed the paper so hard it snapped. She shrank guiltily as annoyed faces turned back to frown her silent. Heaven forbid that she should disturb Professor Austen's more than usually mesmerizing performance!

Darcy felt like a hostess forbidden to eat at her own dinner party. She smouldered in shades of burnt umbrage, keeping uncharacteristically quiet during the long, lively class discussion that followed his presentation.

At ten to four none of the usual rustles anticipating the end of class made themselves apparent. The session went five minutes overtime; Darcy writhed through every additional second as if strapped to Torquemada's personal rack and being slowly stretched even agonizingly taller than nature had made her in the first place.

When the students finally filed out, she rushed down the aisle stairs behind them, hoping to slip out unnoticed among clumps of classmates.

"Miss McGill."

His call was perfectly timed, his tone impeccably impersonal and not to be ignored.

"Yes?" Darcy risked only the quickest of glances at Steven's face. The glasses shielded his expression again, but he seemed to be in complete control as he spoke.

"Could you walk me to my next class? There are some matters I want to talk to you about."

"No!" Her fingers clenched on her pile of texts.

His hand caught her arm bracingly. "Are you feeling all

right? I noticed you were uncommonly quiet in class. And now you strike me as a little pale."

Maybe you're used to painted faces, she wanted to retort, but bit her lip. "I'm just, just in a hurry."

"This won't take long," he said confidently, using the hand still on her arm to guide her into the hallway.

They'd lingered long enough to find the passage deserted by students eager to bolt late-day classes. Darcy felt more alone with Stevenson Eliot Austen than she ever had been, even as Sirene.

They walked without words out of the building into the warm October sunshine. Las Vegas temperatures still reached the high seventies at this time of year, but brisk mornings made the balmy afternoons sweeter by comparison.

"I, ah, feel I must apologize," he said when they were safely under the shade of campus trees set along semiempty sidewalks.

It would have been the epitome of a private academic stroll, except that Darcy's knees were shaking. She felt an imposter; she felt left out of her own love affair. She felt like a liar.

"You apologize?" she heard herself echo at last.

"About—" This wasn't easy for him to say. He shifted the books from under one arm to the other and stared beyond the trees to the doughnut-shaped bulk of the James R. Dickson Library. "About your writing." He stopped to face her. "I didn't understand—about showgirls, about how vital the Strip is to the economic lifeblood of Las Vegas, about life, about your sister, Sirene."

"What are you saying?"

"I'm saying that you shouldn't listen to me." A wan smile, small and wee like E. E. Cummings's balloon man, softened his serious features. "Which you have not done, anyway, thank God. I'm saying that I'm not qualified to judge the subject matter you've chosen to write about. I'm saying that I was narrow-minded, bigoted, an awful prig. You were right and I was wrong. That's all."

A bench had been placed alongside the sidewalk for feebler students—after all, the average age of a UNLV enrollee was twenty-seven. Darcy plunked down on it with none of her customary élan, as abruptly as a lead balloon lands, her books and papers spewing to the seat around her from nerveless arms.

"I've never heard of a teacher apologizing to a student before."

"Perhaps I've been instructed by a good teacher," he said rather wryly, settling beside her. His smile broadened into a dazzling sickle of white teeth that cast a spotlight on the devastating chin dimple. Darcy fought conflicting urges to pinch his cheeks fondly and to knee him in the stomach.

"Won't you be late for your last class?" she asked instead.

He checked his watch. "They'll wait," he concluded with new serenity, all mellow fellow. "I know you've got obligations, too, but I wanted you to know that I had seen the light, so to speak. Mainly, I've come to realize that I misjudged your sister's world. I cherished outmoded stereotypes."

"What triggered this sudden conversion?"

"I saw my first hotel revue, for one thing. Quite a show. And some other . . . things made me think." His hand waved dismissively. "I find it too complicated to explain."

"I bet you do," Darcy muttered.

"What?"

"Nothing. So this means that you—"

"That I was too hasty. I can see that Sirene is the kind of larger-than-life overwhelming personality that might intrigue a writer. I didn't appreciate that at first." A sheepish look munched complacently at his idyllic composure. "In fact, I evolved this theory that you were jealous of Sirene, or trying to live through her."

"You did?" Darcy managed to sound flabbergasted. "Professor, how could you?" she demanded with a touch of impish mirth.

"I know, I know. It's irreprehensible of me." His hands apologetically patted the air between them. "I was blind, but now I see."

"Amazing," she noted.

He glanced sharply at her for signs of sarcasm but saw only a composed, sweetly calm face.

"But you're wrong about Sirene," she added.

"I am? How?" A muscle pulsed anxiously in his cheek.

"She's not what you think she is," Darcy murmured.

His laissez-faire posture stiffened. "Not what I think? Of course, I didn't swallow all that fictional embroidery of yours about amorous Arab sheiks and pursuing high rollers—"

"Oh, *that's* perfectly true. They always hit on showgirls. What's *not* true is that Sirene is as bold and brassy as she appears to be. Actually, she's quite shy."

"Shy?" He choked discreetly, then cleared his throat. "In what way?"

Darcy leveled him with a lengthy hazel stare. "With men."

"With men?"

His voice definitely held a hoarse tone now. Darcy charitably attributed it to too much declaiming in class.

"Well, think about it," she urged. "All those long hours

with the Crystal Phoenix emblem.

"Oh my God. . . ." Darcy let her spine melt against the wall behind her. "Are you a born bluffer or what?"

The deck instantly widened into a fan in his fingers. "Card shark." He smiled tightly. "I work for the hotel as a baccarat referee. I saw these two oiling about the place, then when you came through, I got really curious."

"Why didn't you call security?"

He shrugged, a gesture so slight that it never shifted the fall of the velveteen across his shoulders. "I like to play a lone hand."

Darcy's eyes narrowed. "I know you—you were in this office the other day."

He nodded curtly. "Getting hired. You were hanging around as usual. Why?"

"I work here, too. Dancer. Darcy McGill."

His eyes dropped matter-of-factly to the jeans. "I figured."

"And I'm a good friend of Nicky and Van's. She lets me keep my textbooks in her desk." Darcy ran around to check on the drawer. "Oh no—"

"Busted into?" He had followed and stared with her at the smashed combination lock. "What's in there?"

"Just my stuff! My class books and my, my writing journal!" It suddenly occurred to Darcy how private her written musings were as she took fevered mental inventory of its indicting contents. "Oh, my God—it's gone!"

"Not to worry," came his taut voice behind her. "This it? It was on the desk."

Darcy pressed the poison-green notebook against her chest like a shield. "Yes!"

"What did they really want here?"

"I can't imagine. It sure wasn't Midnight Louie," she

45724

joked, letting her eye caress the calm and flawlessly unruffled cat.

"Who?" the man asked sharply, looking around.

"The cat. Listen, why don't you call security and forget it?"

He was moving briskly through the room, noting the overturned wastebasket, the askew framed prints on the wall. He glanced over his burgundy shoulder, revealing eyes cat-narrow and green.

"Because I'm curious," he replied. "Like a cat."

"I don't know if I should stand by and let you—"

"Smith."

"What?"

"My name is Smith."

"Well, that's hardly reassuring."

He turned to flash a sardonic grin. "They call me Solitaire."

"I can see why."

"Maybe." He seemed undisturbed by her disapproval. "But why were these blackguards searching the office? Bloody funny."

"You're from Australia!" Darcy suddenly remembered.

"Right, mate."

"But your accent isn't totally Aussie," she added suspiciously.

"Hey, Australia's part of the whole wide world nowadays, it's no penal colony anymore. We've got the Americas Cup, after all. You can't expect us to travel the world saying 'Tie me kangaroo down, sport.' "

"Maybe not, but—"

"That's strange."

"What?"

Solitaire Smith, self-christened or not, seemed to know

how to pat down a room. He pulled the big black-and-white desert photo on one wall off its hooks.

"Somebody's been mucking with this," he announced. "It's not a bloody painting; there's no canvas backing to search behind. Strange."

"Are you an amateur detective?"

"I told you; I'm curious. My job is mostly standing around in the baccarat fishbowl and seeing that nobody does anything odd. I can't help it if I see some oddities shambling down the office corridor. And I didn't call security because I prefer to work alone, all right?"

"Why?" Darcy challenged.

"None of your business, Dancer."

"Speaking of strange men . . . I don't know if I like you or not."

He nodded to the notebook. "Better not irritate me or I'll read your diary."

"It's not a diary—it's a writing journal," she said possessively, her arms tightening on it. "Nothing in here would interest you or anybody else."

"I'm sure of the first part," he said dryly. "But something in this room interested somebody else an awful lot. You tell me why."

"This is Las Vegas. It was built by the Mob. No matter how much anybody tries to clean it up, there are a few . . . remnants floating around. Some of them might like to see the Crystal Phoenix crash. Nicky and Van run their own operation."

"Hmmm." His green eyes glinted as dubiously as Midnight Louie's matching ones. "There'd be easier ways to harass a hotel and its owners, for one thing, fomenting a hotel-workers' strike—"

"Nicky and Van pay their employees more than minimum wage, unlike the other hotels. They don't want their guests to have to tip to buy good service. You won't find any more loyal employees from one end of the Strip to the other."

"All right, Miss McGill. I didn't mean to gore your sacred cow. But somebody better tell them what happened."

"I will," said Darcy, sitting at the simple office chair behind Van's broad desk.

Solitaire Smith paused in the doorway. "You're not staying here."

"Sure. That's why I keep my diary—I mean, my journal—here. I write when I'm coming down from a show."

"That wasn't a question. You're not working here anymore, period. It's not safe for young ladies to linger after dark here."

"Who do you think you are?"

Her indignation elicited his first grin, a hard, cautious expression on a face equally as ungiving.

"I told you, ducky. Solitaire Smith's the name. You don't have to believe me, all you have to do is leave. I'll take you to your car, and hurry it up, I can't leave Harry holding a solo spot for much longer."

"You are the most high-handed man," Darcy complained as she joined him at the door with a bewildered frown.

"And you're an outspoken lady who should do what people tell her more often, for her own good. Let's go."

She shrugged her surrender and moved to turn off the light switch. His hand stopped her.

"Leave it on," Solitaire Smith advised with eyes as hard as malachite. "It'll scare the rats away."

In the desert, Steven stretched and yawned. The movement after immobile hours aroused his senses to ignored cramps and the luxury of returning feeling in his feet and behind. Sirene flashed into his mind, or rather the memory of being with Sirene.

He looked at the half-filled page, recognizing the inspiration for the district attorney's headstrong, long, and lovely daughter who was both bright and beautiful. He acknowledged her incarnation in his unconscious, his blending of two near but hopelessly disunited personalities. Fiction was lies, he reflected, and enough lies strung together sometimes amounted to the truth.

On his piled pages, wish and reality blended. Sirene, for all her attractions, merged with a woman who could quote Shakespeare. Fantasy reared its lovely, fey, and consoling head—and it wore the eyes of Darcy McGill.

Steven no longer censored his thoughts but embraced his unlikely heroine and swept with her into the gangsters' stretch Lincoln Continental. The black words stretched limousine-long themselves for line after line, filling page after page until dawn's winged heels rose at his back and kicked their way through his morning windows and into his aching skull like Bruce Lee coming down hard on an errant ninja.

♥ Chapter Twelve ♥

The Last Angry Feline

Naturally, no one thinks to interview Midnight Louie on The Matter of the Two Marauding Footpads. Perhaps I have brought this deplorable inattention upon myself, due to my deeply discreet nature and the fact that I do not wish to blow my cover.

But I was present during the surreptitious searching of Miss Van von Rhine's office and even later the next morning, when Mr. Nicky Fontana finds out and goes stomping from door to window and back, setting down all manner of rules that Miss Van von Rhine has no intention of following, which she conveys by saying like this:

"Now, Nicky darling. I understand your concern, but I will have no guards standing over me while I perform my daily chores. We have had problems with hotel security before, but I am not to be frightened off by a thug or two wandering around in the dark. And, bye the bye, sweetheart, do you not think it was a fine idea that I should hire Mr. Solitaire Smith, since he is such a brave and enterprising fellow as to banish the ruffians and even save our friend, Darcy, from a fate worse than death?"

(I am reporting from memory here and may not have gotten the words exactly right but the meaning is crystal-phoenix clear. Miss Van von Rhine is not the kind of little doll who is to be scared off by anything—man, muscle, or forty-day rainstorm. And that includes husbands.)

Nicky thunders and lightnings a little, but my little doll

(we go back together a long way) keeps telling him no harm is done, except that Darcy should stop using the office at night, and pretty soon everything has blown over, the office is tidied neater than an undertaker's parlor, and Nicky is blowing farewell kisses to his missus and yours truly from the doorway, looking more than somewhat dazed.

So another tempest in a thirteen-story teapot is over and I can get back to contemplating life, which noble pursuit some of the more crass of my critics call snoozing. Since no one asks me, I do not volunteer that the two pieces of flank steak who are tossing Miss Van von Rhine's office have been scouting the hotel for some time.

I suspect them of being hirelings of the notorious Ugly Al Fresco, the most unprincipled hood to darken any door in Vegas. I myself, unobserved in the shadows, have seen these distasteful individuals searching through Mr. Sing Song's pristine kitchen at quiet times and anywhere they can creep unchallenged, which are more places than you can poke a cockroach into—at least in a big joint like a resort hotel.

Not that there is a cockroach to be seen in the Crystal Phoenix, as I consider it part of my unwritten duties to employ free-lance roach patrollers, namely buddies from my old, leaner days on the streets.

These latter are fine mellow fellows; I choose only those who customarily wear white spats or dress in formal black and white for the job, to lend an air of tone to the hotel. They work well and for no more payment than a small gratuity or two in the form of Chef Sing Song's gold reserves, better known as the fish-pond carp. But this is strictly between me and thee, and thee's discretion is somewhat fishy.

So anyway, life goes on as usual at the Phoenix, although I do not think we have seen the last of the strangers who go bump in the night. Mark my words.

And there is one other tidbit of a purely intellectual sort, with which I like to tease my mind during my long moments of meditation in the shade of the poolside palm trees.

For the fact remains that when the bozos rip open Miss Van von Rhine's locked bottom drawer and dredge up Miss Darcy McGill's journal and fling it to the desk, it flips open to a recent entry. Naturally, given my gumshoe instincts, I can not resist skimming the contents. All right; I am insatiably curious.

So I read these entries in my long little doll's large, generous hand and I discover shocking admissions of a personal nature that reveal some ecstasy of recent days and more despair.

And I read one more thing, which no one else can see for the simple fact that Miss Darcy McGill clutches the notebook stingily to her most generous attributes from the moment that she discovers it open on the desk. I read talk of . . . murder . . . most . . . fowl.

♥ Chapter Thirteen ♥

Nicky Fontana and his uncle Mario, six of his brothers—all of them smiling like a cloned cross between John Travolta and an ingratiating shark—and the Fontana family attorney, Walter Maxwell, mutually held up the walls of Van von Rhine's office with their grimly set shoulders.

Van was seated behind the desk and Darcy in front of it. Solitaire Smith leaned against the closed door as if intent on keeping it that way.

"I'm sorry for getting you night shift workers up so early," Van began, glancing at Darcy and Smith.

"Oh, that's all right," chimed the brothers Fontana in unison, their grins widening identically.

Like their youngest member, Nicky, their dark good looks benefitted from snappy dressing in pale, desert colors. Like Nicky, they could take care of themselves and each other.

Unlike Nicky, they had eased naturally into the "Family Business," although exactly what that was they and their unspoken head, uncle Mario, kept from Nicky and Van now that Nicky had become the White Sheep of the Family and ran his hotel strictly on the up and up. But blood was thicker than water, and when troubles boiled around even a legitimate Fontana enterprise, the brothers flocked together like sherbet-suited ravens.

Solitaire Smith shifted uneasily against the door; Family business was Family business. "Look, there's not much more I can tell you, Miss von Rhine," he said tightly. "They were a couple of mangy-appearing blokes. I bluffed them off and they scampered."

"Would they have hurt Darcy if you hadn't been here?"

"I doubt it," Smith answered at the same time as Darcy responded with a shuddered, "Yes!"

"Speakin' of being here—" A young Fontana pushed himself away from the wall to confront Smith with challenge-tightened eyes. "How come a baccarat referee is playin' house detective? I thought Nicky had plenty of legit security staff to do that."

"I see something wrong, I do something about it. Sometimes." Smith answered flatly, his razor-edged features still and dangerous.

Uncle Mario yammered out a few barks meant to represent laughter. "I like your style, Smith. Some of these boys should learn to handle things solo instead of running in a pack all the time."

"I have no style." The smallest of smiles chipped away at Smith's impassive face.

"That's what I mean," uncle Mario said, blowing out a stream of cigar smoke as thick as truck exhaust and squinting shrewd eyes against the irritating results.

In her chair, Darcy writhed and coughed.

"I don't know what we can do about it, Van," she said, eager to escape the confined atmosphere. Nicky's relatives always made her want to avoid spaghetti dinners in quiet, out-of-the-way restaurants. "These burglars got in, they messed up your office, and they left when Solitaire told them to. I was fine; I just happened to be here, although I shudder to think what might have happened if he hadn't been."

"You don't think that it was you they were after?" Nicky had moved behind Van's chair, his manicured hands resting protectively on its back.

"Me? For the love of Nostradamus, who on earth would be after little me?"

Silence greeted Darcy's unequivocal dismissal of that motive.

"What about Van?" a quiet Australian-clipped voice asked behind Darcy.

Brows wrinkled consideringly.

"If someone's out to ruin the hotel," the small man called Maxwell interjected nervously, "she'd be the right place to start. She's the one who pulled it up from vacancy and redesigned the whole thing. Without her, the Crystal Phoenix wouldn't be the classy place it is today." Maxwell glanced apologetically at Nicky. "Not that you didn't contribute your late Grandmother's eight million clean dough from her pasta factory in Venice, California, but let's face it—"

"No argument," Nicky granted. His normally persuasive dark eyes hardened to obsidian. "Without her, Nicky Fontana wouldn't be the classy guy he is today. If anyone's out to get Van, I'll—"

"No one's out to get me." Van stood, a tiny, jasmine-blonde woman who had finally decided to exert her towering internal clout. "I rarely work late." She cast a soft, sapphire-blue glance at Nicky. "Now that we're married," she said pointedly.

In her chair, Darcy smirked to watch her old high school classmate, Nicky Fontana—Mr. Cool—flush. Flush, hell, she amended smugly to herself, Nicky Fontana was blushing! It was nice to know that a woman could still have that effect on a man when married to him, and then she reflected on her own affairs and added her sudden facial heat to his.

"It's obvious what those men wanted," Solitaire Smith interrupted, as if embarrassed by the silence. "They were searching for something."

"But the gaming records and proceeds are kept in the vault downstairs, and guarded around the clock," Van objected. "What on earth could they want in my office?"

"It wasn't Darcy's diary," Smith put in sardonically. "They left that behind."

All eyes focused on Darcy, who responded by going from pink to scarlet in the cheeks.

"It's not a diary! I keep telling people. It's my writer's journal. And they did break into the drawer, but didn't find what they were after—whatever it was."

"Pardon me," Smith said with a curt bow. "As usual Miss McGill has put matters into plain English: No one knows what they were after, but it was something and someone had better find out what it was."

He slid the door open just enough to allow him passage out and slipped into the hall beyond without asking leave or excusing himself.

Fontana Inc. stared after him with flinty eyes.

"I don't like that guy," Ralph, the second youngest, snarled in his most manly voice.

"I do," Van declared, sitting as regally behind her desk as Elizabeth the First among her courtiers.

Uncle Mario winked at her, his nephews shuffled silently—en masse—on Gucci-loafer-shod feet and that was that.

Darcy squirmed. "Can I go now? I don't know anything about anything."

"That doesn't sound promising for a would-be writer," Nicky teased.

"You'll be sorry when you find yourself in my first bestseller," she threatened back with sisterly zeal. "Anyway, I hope you solve the mystery. I gotta get home to grab some z's before I have to show up in class."

She left the office with relief. Such a flocking of Fontanas gave her the willies, for although they were a genteel consortium compared to Vegas' grosser criminal elements, like Ugly Al Fresco's hoods, their clandestine occupation reminded her how intimately the rackets and entertainment entwined the city's history—both past and too possibly present.

Her bronze Nova baked brown in the lot; that was one nice thing about working nights in Las Vegas: you avoided the oven of an asphalt-parboiled car. Darcy gingerly manipulated the steering wheel while the air-conditioner fan blew her streaming hair to kingdom come behind her.

Strange occurrences at the Crystal Phoenix were only peripherally her business, she told herself; every hotel had its minor criminal incidents. Yet she fretted abstractedly on the way home, perhaps because Van had called her at nine that morning when she was used to sleeping until almost noon.

So she was nearly out of her car in the apartment parking lot when she noticed the silver Accord three spaces down. Steven emerged sheepishly as she spotted him.

"How did you—?" she began.

"I found your address in the school records," he said quickly, looking at the asphalt, then checking the length of his nose. It remained perfectly normal despite his blatant falsehood, although Darcy was tempted by a fleeting urge to tweak it.

"I was going to say," she said, "how did you know when I'd be home?"

"I . . . didn't. I've been waiting."

"All morning?"

"Since nine-thirty."

She checked the neat Seiko on her wrist. "It's lunchtime

now and you were in the hot sun all that time? Better come in."

She observed that he looked more rumpled than his usual charming self as she led him up the exterior staircase to her door. She had noticed the hummock of his jacket slung over the Accord's passenger-seat back. His shirt looked like it had lain wet in a dryer for a week, and his slack tie was almost as unstrung as his face.

Steven moved into the shade of the air-conditioned apartment with a sigh. He didn't bother to pretend to admire the decor he was supposedly seeing for the first time, but headed for the wicker settee and sat.

"Coffee, tea, or milk?" Darcy employed a tone of spritely stewardess inquiry.

"Me," he answered absently. "I mean . . . have you any lemonade or club soda or sparkling water?" When she stared at him, he explained. "I'm afraid I didn't get much sleep last night—not any," he amended groggily.

Her knuckles swung impulsively toward his face, which she now saw bristled with the unfocused look of the unshaven, but his own open hand was already stroking the phenomenon.

"Good lord, I even forgot to shave. I'm sorry." He looked up, but she had flounced behind the kitchen divider.

"Don't be," her voice urged from beyond the cabinets. Steven saw her dart down the hall and return, then heard the refrigerator door whoosh open and shut. A hopeful look lightened his heavy sleepless features.

In an instant she had returned to plant a green, long-necked bottle of beer on the cocktail table and cast herself down on the—his writerly mind sought the precise description of this small two-seat unit—on the loveseat, Professor Stevenson Eliot Austen duly noted to himself, wincing.

Darcy elevated a small black item. "If you want to shave later—" He stared, the object coming into focus first, then its meaning. "That's a, a man's electric shaver."

Startled, she froze for a moment. Then the flat of her hand lightly admonished his knee.

"Of course it is, silly! They work better. They're designed to get into all those nooks and crannies, like knobby knees. I use it. On my legs." Something occurred to her. "And . . . Sirene's legs need to be baby-smooth for the show."

"Sirene," he repeated. "One for the money, two for the show, three to get ready, and four to go."

Sirene was a thought that buzzed his brain and then evaporated into the wild blue yonder somewhere over China. Everything seemed seen through a beer bottle, darkly, he thought as he raised the alien libation to his lips. "I seldom drink beer," he commented.

"You need it," Darcy said shrewdly. "Your mind can't get any fuzzier than it is now."

"No," he admitted, slumping back against the plentiful chintz pillows, the beer propped on one slack thigh.

"You look terrible," Darcy said emphatically. "What's wrong?"

Steven ran a hand over his forehead to repel the unruly forelock that had kept tumbling into his eyes on the drive into town. He stared at the beer bottle in his loose grip; it seemed to stare back at him just as glassily.

"I wonder what the university board of regents would think of a professor on their faculty sitting in a student's apartment drinking beer? A female student."

"It's happened before," Darcy snapped. "Steven, what is it? You seem . . . quite unlike yourself, in some altered state. I know you don't drink much, and I can't imagine you smoking cactus root—"

He was smiling the beatific smile of the self-lost; he didn't even notice that Darcy had called him Steven as naturally as if she'd always done it—or dreamed of doing it—or that she seemed to have a more intimate knowledge of his habits than Darcy McGill should.

"You put it well. A writer born," he articulated with weary clarity. " 'An altered state.' I have indeed been so deployed—in an altered state. I was writing."

His toe nudged the briefcase she now noticed on the floor.

"There it is. The foetus of my imagination. It's what I've poured out in the past twelve hours, and it's quite a lot. Funny, I never thought myself garrulous. Anyway, I brought it here because"—he glanced up, the gray eyes murkier than fog—"because I want you to read it to tell me what you think of it."

Darcy took a deep breath. Steven was watching her carefully now, his focus sharpening with every passing second.

"You're the writing professor," she said carefully.

His eyes stayed relentlessly on her face. "This is not professorial scribbling. It's something quite different. Completely out of character. *You*"—the word had an odd emphasis—"were the only one I could think of to show it to, that I would dare show it to. To whom I would dare show it," he rephrased.

"I'm . . . amazed . . . touched," she said, searching for words and finding the precisely right one on the second try. "Steven," she asked, "what's happening to you?"

He shook his head ruefully. "I'm afraid I'm having an 'epiphany'."

"Goodness! Is it fatal?"

He laughed softly. "Artful minx!" he said in the same thrilling theatrical tone with which he read Cavalier poetry aloud. "You know quite well that the word 'epiphany' describes a moment of . . . intense spiritual and emotional enlightenment as depicted in a literary endeavor, in other words, seeing the damn light in black and white!" He leaned forward, instantly energized.

"I've seen it, Darcy! Out on the desert. It knocked me blind. Quaker took me back by himself. I saw that my life, my writing, were just as empty and sterile as all that self-important sand out there. I was drifting, simply drifting, shiftlessly drifting, endlessly rocking."

Darcy caught the beer before it toppled in his hand. Steven's face had fallen sideways onto the sofa pillows, smudges of fatigue mirroring the dark of his lowered eyelashes.

"Why me?" she asked, begged, demanded.

His voice was no more than a drowsy whisper. "I thought that you might understand. I don't."

She reached into the briefcase she had seen so often on his desk, under his desk, swinging from his hand as he strode across campus and she had watched from a distance. She had always watched from a distance, Darcy realized; even Sirene was only a mask to keep that distance intact.

She reached into the dark leather depths and pulled out a sheaf of pale papers, feeling like a violator.

"Are you sure you want me to read this? Steven?"

His eyes remained completely closed, but his lips moved. " 'Ah, Cynara! Last night betwixt her lips and mine there fell thy shadow . . . And I was desolate and sick of an old passion . . .' "

She leaned near to hear it, the brocaded words that made no sense and yet etched ice into her soul.

" 'I have been faithful to thee, Cynara! In my fashion.' "

And then he was asleep. Darcy leaned away from him,

guilty as an imposter who had heard a confession.

The papers trembled slightly in her grasp. Read them? She couldn't. Judge them? Never! What to do? She glanced at his face again.

Darcy's hand delicately pushed the thatch of mahogany hair off his smooth forehead. Sleep had melted away the endearing worry lines. Her fingertip skated along the edge of his jaw. She breathed a careful kiss onto the skin, baby-smooth enough for the treacherous Sirene, behind his earlobe, then stood and surveyed the situation.

The apartment was cool and dark; he was dead to the world and best left sleeping there. She was due at the Crystal Phoenix around six. She could easily kill the time elsewhere.

Darcy bent to ease his feet up over the wicker armrest and took his shoes off. It wasn't the most comfortable position on earth for sleeping, but she wasn't about to try lugging him to the bed. She wasn't *that* big a girl.

"Now, where did you leave your glasses?" she murmured, looking down fondly at her disheveled charge.

He must have had them for driving—of course! Darcy almost snapped her fingers, then stopped herself. The car. She slipped down to the vehicle, luckily left unlocked, and searched the dashboard and glove compartment. Plenty of old parking chits, but no glasses, not even sunglasses. At last she patted the neatly folded jacket with absent recognition and her palm hit pay dirt, a bulky lump in one pocket. Eureka! What a detective! Back in her apartment, she left the folded glasses atop the cocktail table where he'd be sure to see or stumble over them when he awoke. She whisked the mostly full beer bottle back to the kitchen, capped it with aluminum foil, and returned it to the refrigerator.

Her tote bag and purse lay lumpily ready for retrieval by

The Cat and the Queen of Hearts

A Midnight Louie Las Vegas Adventure

Book 2

Carole Nelson Douglas

Five Star
Unity, Maine

Five Star Mystery
Published in conjunction with Tekno Books and Ed Gorman.

December 1999
Standard Print Hardcover Edition.

First Edition, Second Printing

Five Star Mystery Series.

The text of this edition is unabridged.

Set in 11 pt. Plantin by Minnie B. Raven.

Printed in the United States on permanent paper.

Library of Congress Cataloging-in-Publication Data

Douglas, Carole Nelson.
    The cat and the queen of hearts / Carol Nelson Douglas.
    — 1st ed.
        p.   cm. — (A Midnight Louie Las Vegas adventure ; bk. 2)
(Five Star mystery series)
    ISBN 0-7862-2173-9 (hc : alk. paper)
    I. Title. II. Series.
PS3554.O8237 C245   1999
    813'.54—dc21   99-046904

For Melinda Helfer—whose dedication to books, readers, and writers is matched only by her insight and sensitivity—with deepest thanks for advice and encouragement, and for being the first reviewer (but not the last) to predict that readers would want more of Midnight Louie

♥ Author's Foreword ♥

This is the second of the four books comprising the Midnight Louie Quartet. These books—written in 1985–86, finally published two to a volume as *Crystal Days* and *Crystal Nights* in 1990, and until now out of print—feature Midnight Louie, whose current mystery series has eleven books in print (*Catnap, Pussyfoot, Cat on a Blue Monday, Cat in a Crimson Haze, Cat in a Diamond Dazzle, Cat with an Emerald Eye, Cat in a Flamingo Fedora, Cat in a Golden Garland, Cat in a Hyacinth Hunt, Cat in an Indigo Mood,* and *Cat in a Jeweled Jumpsuit*). The interior alphabet that began with *Blue Monday* means there will ultimately be 27 books in the series.

The current Midnight Louie mystery series shares the same Las Vegas setting as the earlier books, but reflects the city's incredible building boom of the past 14 years (to which I have added fictional hotel-casinos, like the Crystal Phoenix and the Goliath that feature in the Quartet). Many of the secondary characters and the backgrounds from the Quartet continue in the current series, forming a continuing universe, and the Quartet is the entire reason the Midnight Louie mystery series exists at all.

When the Quartet was sold to a category romance line in 1985, it was one of the first limited series within a romance line, and was the first to feature a feline PI narrator and include crime and mystery elements, anticipating trends that have become bestsellers since then. The romance editor enthusiastically bought the Quartet and received the first manuscript. Then something happened. The books were held from publication for four years, so long that the con-

7

tract expired. During that time, I was promised various publishing dates and methods of publishing—the first book in hardcover, for instance—that never came about. A clue to the delay was in the editor's description of the books: "too mainstream, upmarket, and sophisticated" for romance readers. Finally, the editor promised that the books would be well published and I would be pleased, and that they would be out within a year.

They came out in the summer of 1990, not in the romance line, but as midlist romances. And I was not pleased. The editor had crammed the four books into two paperbacks containing two stories each. The 120,000-word length of the doubled-up books wasn't economical, so the editor cut each book up to 37 percent without my knowledge or participation. (I call the approach "cutting the body to fit the coffin.") I wouldn't have seen galley proofs had I not asked for them, and did all I could then to salvage the books. They did not meet my standards: plot elements seemed pulled out of the blue without preparation, mystery elements and deeper characterizations were stripped out, as were secondary characters. Forty percent of the Midnight Louie sections were cut.

Convinced that the very elements the romance editor found "too upmarket, mainstream, and sophisticated"— Midnight Louie's narration, the Las Vegas setting, and the mystery/romance blend—were strengths, not weaknesses, and infuriated by this unprofessional treatment from a major house, I "flipped" the concept and took Louie to the mystery side of the street, where he has been welcome indeed. Midnight Louie, after all, is based on a real alley cat with awesome survival skills. He weighed eighteen pounds from eating a California motel's decorative goldfish, which almost got him sent to the animal Death Row before a cat-

lover flew him to her home fifteen hundred miles away to save him.

I am grateful for the reader interest that makes it possible for the Midnight Louie Quartet to return in a restored form the author can endorse. In preparing the Quartet books for publication, I restored material that had been cut, including all of Louie's narrative sections. These were always briefer than they are in the current mystery series. Just having a cat narrator was daring enough in 1985–86; I made sure to keep his contributions short, if not sweet. Since the books were written as romances first, the mystery/crime elements are lighter than in the mystery series, but they are there, and involve a continuing puzzle that isn't solved until the last book.

Las Vegas has changed so much, so fast, and so radically since I researched and wrote this book in 1985 that I'm leaving the background "as was" to record what it used to be like. Because of the fast-forward nature of the Las Vegas scene, this is the pattern of the Midnight Louie mystery series too. The characters in the foreground move through a time period of months while the background buildings whiz by, reflecting years of construction and de-construction. It's like the early movies where the actors played a scene in an unmoving car while a montage of background scenes flew by. That's the only sensible way to deal with The City That Won't Stop Reinventing Itself.

So here comes the Quartet again, in a new "authorized" edition.

The credit for the revival goes, in the end, to readers who live long, and don't forget. In that way, they're a lo like Midnight Louie, the alley cat who wouldn't die.

♥ Chapter One ♥

"Visitors aren't allowed backstage, Sir," she pointed out, dabbing her chin with a makeup sponge.

The Arab prince stood behind her. The snowy whiteness of his traditional headdress haloed a swarthy face. His eyes, matched black falcons, soared among the distantly glimpsed peaks of his emotions.

She leaned closer to the mirror. Along its edges ran a haphazard frame of snapshots, postcards and notes written in lipstick. She knew why the Emir of Abba Dhabba's son was in her dressing room, even though he shouldn't have been. Rules meant nothing to a prince used to ruling exotic Arabian nights and shifting desert sands.

"I bribed the guard." His fingers fanned magician-like to produce what appeared to be a one-dollar bill tailed by a tight train of three zeroes.

Her eyes, a soft hazel shade, yet as fierce in their way as the man's darker ones, met his in the mirror.

"You paid too much. Usually a fifty will do it."

His shrug emphasized the voluminous robes draping his figure. "It matters not. What does matter is that it is necessary for you to call me Highness."

She pushed back her chair, its legs grating across the makeup-tatooed concrete floor, and rose slowly. Her body seemed to uncoil forever in stages of calculated grace—after all, she was a dancer and nearly six feet tall without high heels on.

This night she still wore the two-and-a-half-inch-heeled silver T-strap pumps from her turn on stage. The dim lights high above stirred subtle glitter among the swags of rhinestones draping her torso. She rose and rose, like a curtain, finally looking down on her would-be suitor.

She smiled and complied dutifully with the custom of the desert kingdom.

"Yes, *Highness*." She put a certain emphasis on the title that even a prince couldn't afford to overlook.

Throwing the thousand-dollar bill onto the cluttered dressing table, the Emir of Abba Dhabba's son drew his desert robes around himself like a cape and swirled toward the dressing room door.

"I have not finished with you," he threatened before his exit, with all the deep passion that dwells in a vastly spoiled youth of twenty-four.

Sirene sat again, more slowly than she had risen, and turned back to the mirror. She plucked up the discarded thousand-dollar bill between the pincers of inch-and-a-half-long fingernails, kicked out one long dancer's leg for the hell of it, and thrust the bill into the fragile custody of her flesh-colored net and rhinestone bra.

"*This*," she vowed, "is as close as you'll ever get . . . Highness."

"Well." Professor Stevenson Eliot Austen stopped reading and cleared his throat, in that order.

His creative writing class sat rapt, chins braced on fists, eyes wide. The mesmerizing Austen baritone could make a yawn sound impressive, but for once his subject matter was equally exciting.

Outside a wall of windows the sage-colored olive trees

Despite their flattery, the boys had ended up escorting the other three queens around Vegas, sans Darcy. She went home to bed at one o'clock in the morning, as she usually did, and smiled tolerant disinterest at the others' tales of the night before and morning after.

Now Darcy grinned at Midge before bending over to pull on cellophane-sheer tights. Two more opposite-looking women would be hard to find in a radius of four hundred miles. Yet the face Midge expertly erected in the mirror blurred their differences. By the time Darcy straightened and began looking around for the wig for her first production number, the Midge in the mirror seemed her spitting image.

"The professor kept me after class," Darcy admitted while dressing—or rather, while undressing.

"But it's working out okay?" The new speaker had just rushed through the doors, pulling along a redheaded woman—also long, tall, and handsome—Jo. "Lordy, you two early birds! We better move our behinds."

"Yes, girls, it's working out okay." Darcy flexed a long leg to the chair seat while she buckled on the standard-issue T-strap dancing pumps, which looked clunky but were at least safe. "The instructor is old-school. Most punctilious," she added in mock-British accents.

"Listen to the girl swear! That's what higher education'll get you, huh, Trish?"

Trish, a big-boned redhead in a shapeless smock, was busy transforming herself into an onstage persona as sleek and glamorous as those with a head-start around her. For now she was pawing among small jars of theatrical makeup and cursing the colorful globs that oozed under her long false fingernails.

"That's why I put mine on last," Darcy couldn't help

crowing as she sat calmly applying her own mandarin-long, Chinese-red talons.

"Someday you'll forget and go on nail-less, and then Danny Dove will have your hide, whether you're a friend of the management or not," said the towering blonde in fishnet tights.

"Look, Jo; if you want to go through life two-inches distant from everything you touch, fine. I don't see how you dial a phone."

"Dah-ling, I don't." Jo pencilled a perfect eyebrow into an even more exaggerated arch. "I have Touch-tone, don't you?"

"No, but has that got something to do with your boyfriend, the California masseur?"

Pantyhose descended on Darcy's bent head. "Watch it, kids," she warned, "if I get anything in this glue before it's tacky—"

"Very tacky," Midge observed, removing Jo's flung pantyhose and squinting critically at Darcy's glue-glazed nails. "If those things don't set by showtime, they'll go flying off during your costume changes like old piano ivories. It could be a public hazard backstage."

"You three are a public hazard." Darcy groaned. "This timetable has gotta work. The whole reason I enrolled at UNLV is Professor Austen's creative writing course. How'd I know it was scheduled for the second-to-last time slot of the day?"

"A stodgy old academic type is worth risking your genuine false Coquette-of-Hollywood nails—with batch-blended glitter? Some people have warped values," Jo lectured.

Darcy paused to consider while her faux nails and original issue fingertips dried—hopefully—till death or Nail Undo did them part.

under the hot glare of spotlights, their garish makeup washed out to near-pallor, their smiles at full candlepower, and their flashing feet dancing their hearts and soles out.

Darcy was last to hurtle up to the mirrored offstage door that offered an eleventh-hour costume check to every racing dancer who pounded past it.

She looked uncannily like all the rest: a tall, elongated figure of mostly unclad female beauty, rhinestone G-string sparkling, rhinestones draping her bikini bodice and entwining every extremity—and some areas that weren't even extremities—ankles, wrists, upper arms, throat, and forehead. Dotted like stars through the vivid artificial curls of her scarlet wig, twinkled a galaxy of even more . . . rhinestones. If only "stodgy" old Professor Austen could see her now!

Darcy winked back at her glittering reflection and rammed her palms into the door, pushing her way through the cluttered dark backstage and then onto the sun-bright dazzle of the bare stage beyond, so small and earthbound to support so large and celestial a constellation of begemmed bodies on the hoof.

Maribu-feather snowflakes floated in spotlight beams. A hundred dancing feet drummed up a racket that never floated past the footlights. The surging melodies from the orchestra pit and the pre-recorded chorus singing for their supper drowned out all else while the onstage dancers strutted.

The show ran an hour and forty minutes, but Darcy always said it felt like it lasted one full quarter of football—without time-outs. The fifty chorus members averaged thirty complete costume changes, and the women often were saddled with elaborate headdresses that weighed enough to make Angel Cordero cringe.

"He's not really stodgy, but funny in a dry sort of way. And not old at all. Thirty-something, I'd guess."

"Single?" Trish asked with a rising note of interest in her voice.

Darcy flushed under her pancake, but the half-moons of blusher she'd painted under her cheekbones remained the only red visible on her face besides lipstick.

"I don't really know," she said distantly. "That's not what I'm at UNLV to learn."

Trish shrugged as she writhed into her tights. "There must be scads of men on campus, but they're probably the dull type."

Midge, who had recently remarried, smiled benignly.

"Dull," Darcy concurred, rising to whisk a carrot-colored wig of sausage curls off the Styrofoam wig block. She made a face at the frozen white features, which some idle chorus girl or boy had meticulously made up to match her own.

"Hey, they stayed on!" Darcy pulled the wig over her flattened hair and flashed ten red talons under her room-mates's well-powdered noses.

"Wait'll you try to peel out of the metallic snake outfit in thirty seconds at the end of Act II," Midge predicted. "That'll be the real test."

Darcy, ready first, just grinned and waited for the others to abandon the comfortable clutter of their dressing tables.

The "squawk box," a small speaker with a kitetail of wire long enough to broadcast onstage sound down to their dressing room so the dancers could hear their cues, busily regurgitated pre-opening racket. "Ten minutes," the stage manager's put-upon tones declared. "Places, people."

Jo, Midge, Darcy, and Trish joined the stream of choru girls clattering up the backstage steps to burst on stag

33

"He's not really stodgy, but funny in a dry sort of way. And not old at all. Thirty-something, I'd guess."

"Single?" Trish asked with a rising note of interest in her voice.

Darcy flushed under her pancake, but the half-moons of blusher she'd painted under her cheekbones remained the only red visible on her face besides lipstick.

"I don't really know," she said distantly. "That's not what I'm at UNLV to learn."

Trish shrugged as she writhed into her tights. "There must be scads of men on campus, but they're probably the dull type."

Midge, who had recently remarried, smiled benignly.

"Dull," Darcy concurred, rising to whisk a carrot-colored wig of sausage curls off the Styrofoam wig block. She made a face at the frozen white features, which some idle chorus girl or boy had meticulously made up to match her own.

"Hey, they stayed on!" Darcy pulled the wig over her flattened hair and flashed ten red talons under her roommates's well-powdered noses.

"Wait'll you try to peel out of the metallic snake outfit in thirty seconds at the end of Act II," Midge predicted. "That'll be the real test."

Darcy, ready first, just grinned and waited for the others to abandon the comfortable clutter of their dressing tables.

The "squawk box," a small speaker with a kitetail of wire long enough to broadcast onstage sound down to their dressing room so the dancers could hear their cues, busily regurgitated pre-opening racket. "Ten minutes," the stage manager's put-upon tones declared. "Places, people."

Jo, Midge, Darcy, and Trish joined the stream of chorus girls clattering up the backstage steps to burst on stage under the hot glare of spotlights, their garish makeup washed out to near-pallor, their smiles at full candlepower, and their flashing feet dancing their hearts and soles out.

Darcy was last to hurtle up to the mirrored offstage door that offered an eleventh-hour costume check to every racing dancer who pounded past it.

She looked uncannily like all the rest: a tall, elongated figure of mostly unclad female beauty, rhinestone G-string sparkling, rhinestones draping her bikini bodice and entwining every extremity—and some areas that weren't even extremities—ankles, wrists, upper arms, throat, and forehead. Dotted like stars through the vivid artificial curls of her scarlet wig, twinkled a galaxy of even more . . . rhinestones. If only "stodgy" old Professor Austen could see her now!

Darcy winked back at her glittering reflection and rammed her palms into the door, pushing her way through the cluttered dark backstage and then onto the sun-bright dazzle of the bare stage beyond, so small and earthbound to support so large and celestial a constellation of begemmed bodies on the hoof.

Maribu-feather snowflakes floated in spotlight beams. A hundred dancing feet drummed up a racket that never floated past the footlights. The surging melodies from the orchestra pit and the pre-recorded chorus singing for their supper drowned out all else while the onstage dancers strutted.

The show ran an hour and forty minutes, but Darcy always said it felt like it lasted one full quarter of football—without time-outs. The fifty chorus members averaged thirty complete costume changes, and the women often were saddled with elaborate headdresses that weighed enough to make Angel Cordero cringe.

Darcy's major moment came during the "Royal Suite Revue," the closing number that revolved around, quite literally, an onstage, multi-tiered carousel on which she, Jo, Trish, and Midge descended flights of curving stairs without one downward glance, each dressed as one of the queens from a deck of cards.

Darcy's costume was composed of scarlet satin hearts as small as possible yet still capable of covering illegal areas of the anatomy. Her red satin T-strap shoes never faltered on the slippery black Plexiglas stairway unit, far more sure-footed than her low heels had been descending Professor Austen's classroom steps. That was life, she reminded herself: one was permitted to stumble. This is show biz.

Her arms, flung wide and coiled with bits of lace and glitter and swagged strings of pearls, never veered from their graceful shoulder-height position. Her slender neck never trembled under the burden of felt, glue, maribu, pearls, and glitter that unfurled from her head like an Aztec king's headdress.

While she smiled serenely and glided from shining step to shining step, Darcy often considered that a Las Vegas showgirl had one thing in common with a downtrodden Third-World housewife—a stiff neck.

She smiled into the spotlights and let the distant rumble of applause wash lightly past her. Then the high rose-velvet curtain clapped its severed folds together with silent finality, and they had an hour before the next show, when they had to do it all over again.

"Hey, the nails did okay!" Midge paused to approve Darcy's intact claws while wriggling out of her sable satin Queen-of-Spades ensemble in the dressing room.

Darcy had already exchanged the intricacies of her Queen-of-Hearts costume for blue jeans and sweatshirt when three frantic stagehands barreled through the high double doors as a short cut to the scenery shop.

"Do you mind?" Trish, attired in little more than she had come into the world wearing, voiced her objection in an outraged treble.

The blasé stagehands leered on cue and blundered on.

"That's the worst part about our 'private' dressing room; it used to be public and everyone in the show still treats it that way," Jo fumed. "I wish there was a nice way to tell those guys to buzz off!"

"Hey, I know." Darcy pulled a lined notebook from the carry-all at her bare feet. "I'll write a 'Keep Out' notice."

"Any of us could have done that." Jo's fists rested on her sturdy hips. "Chorus girls can spell, you know."

"I know, and swear, too." Darcy was already jotting sentences down in her notebook. "But can you make a cherry pie? Don't sweat it. I'll have this done by opening number of the next show. Drat these nails! A person could commit hara-kiri just trying to write her name, not to mention deathless . . . well, you'll see."

By the beginning of the second show the other three women did see, and by the next day so did a lot of would-be trespassers.

In fact, after Midge tacked up a photograph that showed four Victorian nudes of rather rotund dimensions reclining among their draperies, the dressing room door became a favorite showpiece with which chorus members dazzled out-of-towners and visiting relatives. But nevermore did an uninvited guest enter.

"That Darcy," the word went around, "she sure has a clever way with words."

Darcy enjoyed her sub-stage literary reputation, but was glad that Professor Stevenson Eliot Austin was in no position to ever read her rhymes.

Under the title, "This is your Final Warning; enter at your own risk," ran these simple but effective quatrains:

"We are the tallest in the show,
We have the smallest room.
You use it as a corridor,
Is this to be our doom?

"And so we're asking you, our friends,
To let us have our space.
And if you don't, the nudes will have
To rearrange your face.

"So no hard feelings, everyone,
You know we love you all.
We can't help it if our legs are long;
Our mothers made us tall."

♥ Chapter Three ♥

An Interjection from an Old Acquaintance Who Should Not Be Forgot

Of course there is one individual who is always welcome in the oldest established temporary floating dressing room in Vegas, which is inhabited by the four queens. (No connection with the hotel of that name in beautiful downtown Las Vegas, other than all being good-looking dolls whether displayed on pasteboard or the stage boards.)

And naturally, I make the most of any opportunity to rush in where angels fear to tread, especially in the pursuit of my duties as unofficial house dick at the finest little hotel ever to make the Las Vegas Strip sizzle like a New York steak. I speak of the Crystal Phoenix Hotel and Casino, a name which no doubt is familiar to you, as it is to every well-travelled sojourner in the United States of America as well as several lands of a distant variety around the globe.

Perhaps my name has escaped you; that is not entirely bad. I prefer to keep a low profile. But out on the Strip, where the action goes up as the sun goes down, they call me Midnight Louie. Not everyone knows my true identity and those that do keep their lips zipped. Among my intimates I number Nostradamus, one of the more astute bookies to grace a phone booth, although he has the distasteful habit of speaking in rhyme.

In this he has much in common with Miss Darcy McGill, who aspires to be a word-slinger, it is well known, and has and skedaddling, was sure the exact opposite was true. She leaned toward the mirror-posted note, squinting as if reading runes rather than the confidently illegible writing that slanted across the paper in fat, fuzzy lead marks indicative of a pencil in urgent need of sharpening.

But she could learn no more than the three little words that Jo had revealed originally. *Steven. Eliot. Austen.* Steven? Of course! He was calling on the notorious Sirene and didn't want to intimidate her by using the full "Stevenson"—or he simply hoped to disguise his respectable identity.

Darcy let the note go even fuzzier as her eyes brought her adjacent mirror image into sharp focus. "I look like a Flora Dora girl," she wailed.

"That's the general idea, hon." Midge passed Darcy with a consoling shoulder pat as she left, eager to get home to husband (new) and kids (old).

"Who *is* this guy?" Trish already had eeled into stirrup slacks almost as formfitting as her tights, then tied on a red-print bandanna that clashed gloriously with her Titian hair.

"Nobody!" Darcy assured her so quickly that even Steven Eliot Austen would have objected had he been present.

"Oh." Trish nodded knowingly. "No money, huh? Well, dump him quick. I gotta run. Grocery shopping."

Two A.M. was prime time for busy showgirls to attend to mundane matters, and Las Vegas food markets stayed open, like casinos, around the clock. Most of them even offered slot machines for gambling-happy shoppers.

In the dressing room, Jo remained behind.

"What shall I do?" Darcy wondered plaintively.

"Tell Jake ixnay on letting the guy down here. Or whip off that gook and see him." She paused behind Darcy's chair on her way out. "And be prepared to tell Auntie Jo all tomorrow night before the show."

On that ominous advice, the last of the three queens abdicated the dressing room, leaving Darcy chaperoned by rows of feathered costumes softly nodding in the breeze from the air conditioning vent—and a drowsing black cat curled artfully on a crimson velvet pillow.

"Oh, Louie, what should I do? He may already know that I'm . . . I'm—me!"

Semi-slit green eyes widened to display supreme disinterest in the proceedings.

"Unless—" Darcy leaned into the mirror, scrutinizing her features. The Queen-of-Hearts makeup was even more extravagant than her base face. Crimson hearts rouged each cheek, a heart-shaped rhinestone did duty as a beauty mark on her chin, and her lips wore a red Cupid's bow that outshot Love's Leading Archer himself.

If only Jake hadn't already spilled the beans . . . even now he might be talking to the man!

Darcy raced for the hall, her high heels ringing manically on unadorned concrete. Quiet stalked the normally frenetic corridors where fire hoses and drinking fountains passed for wall decorations; bone-beat dancers didn't linger after the ball was over in Las Vegas. Near the pay phone with its scribbled carona of graffiti, Darcy punched Jake's extension into the house phone used only for business.

"Jake? This is . . . Miss McGill. Send Mr. Austen down, with good directions, please."

"Oh, going formal, are we? Very good, Madame," Jake rasped back with just enough sarcasm for only Darcy to detect.

She clattered back to her dressing room niche to unpin her long brown hair. Daytime, and on campus, she wore it in a tight bun. For shows, she pinned it any which way. But Steven was coming—now, at least, she knew what he called himself outside class. *Steven.* . . . Darcy whimpered with urgency, then steeled herself. Think. Why was he here? Because he must . . . care. About Darcy. Therefore, she *had* to see him. But wait! She mustn't let him see her like this . . . it would ruin everything! Which was nothing.

She made herself concentrate on one thing at a time. *Steven.* No, her hair. Or . . . Sirene's hair. Of course. Steven must see what he expected to see. Sirene. Steven . . . and Sirene. And Darcy? *Forget Darcy,* she told herself savagely. You painted yourself into this little corner, honey, and now you can just rely on a little paint to get yourself out of it. At least she would see Steven after hours, talk to Steven, even if he didn't recognize her. And he wouldn't, not if it were in her power to spare him disillusionment.

So, her hair. She needed an updo that would suit the sophisticated Sirene. Playing with recalcitrant ribbons of fine brown hair occupied her mind and fingers until an unmistakable shadow filled the doorway.

"Excuse me. Miss McGill?"

Darcy spun around as if wildly surprised. And she was—to hear him address Darcy and yet not address Darcy.

"I'm afraid we haven't met," she blurted. Best to instill that idea from the outset!

He crossed the threshold as if stepping over a live power line. His shoes were so polished, they looked wet, but he was still wearing the tweedy jacket, now accoutered with a button-down shirt and a gray-wool tie.

"I'm, uh, an instructor of your sister's." It occurred to him she might have more than one. "Your twin sister, Darcy."

"That's all there is," she answered brightly. The fewer

members of this make-believe family, the better. "You must be from the university campus. I never get over there, but it looks pretty with all those trees and things."

"Yes, yes." He sidled into the room, his eyes roaming as inconspicuously as possible over the busy accumulation of costuming and cosmetics. "Lots of trees"—his gaze rested on Midge's rhinestone bikini, hung graphically from her now-dark makeup lights—"and things. Er, Miss McGill—"

"Sirene to you," she insisted nervously. "Steve, is it? Any friend of Darcy's is a friend of mine."

"I'm not precisely a friend. I'm an instructor," he clarified. "But I am interested in her education. She shows remarkable writing talent."

"Oh." Darcy thrilled to hear him praise her to someone else. Sort of. Sirene reasserted herself. "Yeah, that's Darcy," came out carelessly. "Always scribbling things down. Even gets fancy with the grocery list. I mean, you'd think she could write down 'peas,' but no, it's gotta be 'Green Giant frozen LeSeuer baby peas,' you know? It doesn't surprise me she's good at English."

He smiled privately and her heart plummeted. "Creative writing and English are hardly the same thing, Miss McGill."

"No, but they're peas in a pod, right, Professor?" she quipped. "Kinda like Darcy and me. Twins." Darcy/Sirene was slipping into firm character now. All she needed was a wad of chewing gum. It was kind of fun, even a bit liberating, to pretend to be somebody who didn't have to hide how she felt all the time. Someone who had never been shy. "So what can I do for you?" Sirene inquired genially, rising to lean her bare hips against the dressing table.

The gray eyes followed her motion with well-concealed disbelief. "If I've come at a bad time, I can call again, at your convenience. But I didn't want Darcy to know and didn't know what hours you kept—"

Sirene's self-mocking laugh interrupted him, and surprised the heck out of Darcy. "It ain't banker's hours, Doc—or aren't you one?"

"No, I have a Ph.D."

"Well, have a seat too." She pulled out the light bentwood chair from Midge's table.

He turned to eye the seat's faint dusting of silver glitter interspersed with a vagrant maribu feather, then sat with grim resolve.

"Did you see the show?" Darcy whisked her chair around so the back faced him, then straddled it limberly, her arms resting along the curved top.

Professor Austen's chair's legs groaned across the concrete as his settling-in motions bucked it and himself back a bit.

"Yes." He raised the oversize folder he had been clutching like a gaudy prayer book. Darcy, who was used to seeing him accompanied by books and papers, recognized the menu-sized show program. "My first Las Vegas show, actually."

"How long have you lived here?" she asked.

"All my life, but—"

"Oh, I know. You're one of these hoity-toity intellectuals who think the only dancing that's arty is done in toe shoes by girls who look like they're wearing tulle dusters for skirts and guys in pink tights."

"On the contrary, I think some modern dance, Denis Shawn, for instance, is—"

Red satin shoes tapped him into silence. "Well, let me tell you, Doc, that toe-shoe routine can damage a girl's anatomy, plus you have to starve yourself half to death. This

Vegas footwork takes just as much skill, and some of the costumes we wear are a damn-sight heavier than tulle."

He studied the length of her splayed white legs. Sitting as she was, with most of what there was of her costume obscured, she probably looked as if she were clothed by only the shadows cast by the curved latticework of her chair.

"Your anatomy looks quite undamaged and relatively unstarved, if I may say so, Miss McGill."

"Sirene," she insisted sharply. It wouldn't do to have him confusing her with Darcy. "And thank you." She preened, arching her back and lifting a hand to the gleaming hair coiled cobra-like atop her head.

Professor Austen's eyes did not move to her head.

"What I'm here for," he began in much the same portentous tone in which he opened the first class of the semester, "is to discuss your sister—her writing, actually, but that begins with her, and it's she I'm concerned about."

"It's *she*. Sheesh! Yeah?"

Sirene spun her chair back to the mirror and began patting her face with a powder puff. Her profile seemed to put Professor Austen at ease.

"Yeah," he answered a bit more aggressively. "I'm afraid that your example—your somewhat flamboyant lifestyle, that is—is having a detrimental effect on Darcy."

"No kidding?" Sirene spun around again to pinion his diffident eyes with a see-through gaze. " 'Detrimental.' Is that like dandruff?"

He ignored her response and pointed triumphantly at her face, as if relieved. "I see it now! Your eyes are *blue*. That's the difference!"

Darcy was shocked. He believed in Sirene so much he had misinterpreted her eyeshadow for the color of her eyes. He was, as usual, seeing only what he wanted to see. Maybe

. . . maybe *Steven* would like *Sirene* better than Darcy. Maybe she should really *be* Sirene. It was no sooner thought than some imp in Darcy drew Sirene even further forward. And Sirene was very forward indeed.

"What color are Darcy's eyes?" she asked, lowering blue-shaded lids modestly.

"Hazel," he answered promptly. "A remarkably clean, sharp hazel, bright as water-polished agates."

"My, you are a writing professor, Doc. You go on just like Darcy," Sirene cooed admiringly. Inside Sirene, Darcy melted like hot fudge. She desperately wanted to claw her way out and receive the compliment in person.

Instead, she stood, knowing she looked, in all her feathered, satin-and-pearl glory, like a figure from an Erté print.

The professor, recognizing a new boldness in what he perceived as sufficiently bold already, leaned back as if from a fire. But the shockingly small bits of red satin advanced recklessly as Sirene gyrated toward him.

"What color are *your* eyes?" she inquired softly.

Suddenly she kicked a leg over his head and straddled him as if he were a chair, her long legs splitting to support her weight on his lap. A red-nailed hand moved to his temple, then wrenched his glasses away.

"Wait a minute! I need those to see!"

He reached after them but her arm—long, white and gracefully in command—planted them well out of reach on the dressing table.

Professor Stevenson Eliot Austen felt the balance of power let him down with a jolt.

"Gray," she answered herself, gazing into his eyes. "I don't have any fancy words for them, but it's a very nice gray."

Her forefinger, dipped in a bloody talon, traced a path down the middle of his face, from hairline to nose to the channel above his lips. It skipped his mouth and came to rest, pointedly, in the small depression in his chin that his mother had called a dimple when he was a baby, and that he had avoided calling attention to ever since.

"You know, Professor, you're really quite a nice-looking man without your glasses." Her taloned fingers disported at his temples and the back of his neck. "If you'd just relax; you know, get the wind and the rain in your hair, loosen your tie. . . ."

Devilishly agile fingers were fussing at the knot under his Adam's apple, which was engaged in the urgent task of bobbing for saliva or breath or both. Some preylike paralysis ensnared him.

"Now see here, Sirene—"

"Oh, I do see." Her voice lowered as her hands slipped inside his jacket. "You're in good shape. Racquetball?"

"Tennis," he corrected automatically, staring into the red-white-and-blue features that hovered over his with narcotic effect. He felt like a thrush entoiled in the embrace of a rather patriotic snake.

"Ummm, tennis. I just love tennis," Sirene gurgled breathlessly. "All that lunging and glistening sweat." Sirene's face was on a collision course with his. He stiffened as her lips—red and sinfully glossed, nibbled along his.

"You have a delicious mouth," she was murmuring. "I love to watch your lips when you talk. Has anyone ever told you that?"

"Ummf, no. I can't say they . . . er, he . . . um, she— grammatically, Miss McGill, as well as physically, you have pushed me into a corner."

"Awwww." Her regret sounded distinctly like the falling of crocodile tears.

She eased back for a moment so he could attempt to focus on what was happening, on her face. For a mad moment he saw hazel superimposed on blatant blue. Before he could separate reality from surprising fantasy, she swooped voraciously toward him again.

This time her lips met his squarely, pre-meditatively.

He grasped her arms tightly, hesitated, then repelled her with the same strength it took to ram a low serve over the net. She was stronger than he had thought. It was as much her willingness as his insistence that eventually loosened her grip.

He opened his eyes, closed against the recent assault, cautiously. This was worse. His grip on her arms had forced her breasts into a condition of cleavage usually confined to racy men's magazines, and he had pushed her away only enough to present this rather obvious display right under his nose, more than metaphorically speaking.

"Please, Miss—" He couldn't call her that, he thought vaguely, not after this. "Please, Sirene. I came here to talk about your sister. Now." He assumed a fierce tone used for dealing with a classroom disciplinary problem. "Give me back my glasses."

She looked down at him, her hazel/blue eyes limpid, her mouth pouting sensually, then plunked the glasses sulkily into his open palm.

"Now get up."

She did it by simply straightening her endlessly long legs, so that she straddled him like the unfortunate statue of Goliath outside the even more unfortunate hotel of that name. Hands on naked hips, she tilted her head and stared down at him.

"Now, step back."

She complied. "Is this a game? Kind of like Steven Says?"

Any straw in a storm, he thought, berating himself for mixing metaphors. "Yes, a game. Steven Says change into your street clothes."

"Okay." Her compliant hands went to the slender ropes of pearls swagging her hips.

"Steven Says—wait!"

Her hands dropped obediently but her eyes held a wicked twinkle.

"Steven Says, er, change after I'm gone. I'll wait outside the door."

Outside, he paced, studying expanses of mint-green walls interrupted by gray-steel circuit boxes as if their homeliness conferred an aesthetic satisfaction beyond price. Far down the hall, the canvas-swathed ghosts of costumes hung on pegs ready for the next show, hunched unhappily.

Steven pushed up his jacket sleeve to read the Timex's plain face. Two o'clock. In the morning. He must be dreaming. Why on earth had he left a perfectly pleasant, decorous faculty party early to come to this, this—he glanced around—this bunker of iniquity, this sequined sepulchre, this web for the unwary?

He opened the program again, immediately accosted by the vision of a lush female form attired in a tracery of sequins, the glare of the spotlights and that's all. He studied the face; it didn't seem to be Sirene's, but then they all looked alike once properly—or improperly, that is—painted.

Spinning to make yet another pointless stalk in a new direction, Steven found himself nose-to-nose with a posted note. Not a note, a quatrain, the academic in him corrected. Three of them, in fact. He read them, merely because presented with written word, whether by W. H. Auden or the

choreography clattered them together again.

"You what?" Trish squeaked indignantly.

"I . . . borrowed . . . your . . . dress."

"My special zorchy number? That Austen guy must be something special."

"Wrong. He's just my English professor."

They tapped together in perfect, mechanical harmony while Danny Dove beamed upon the entire chorus line's apparent industriousness.

"I love the way Englishmen talk," Trish mused when their roles had subsided to muted rapping at the back of the stage while a quartet performed flashier maneuvers up front. "So why'd you need my hypertension dress?" Trish finally turned in a choreographed circle, her back to Danny.

Darcy sighed. "Because he didn't know I was me. And he isn't English, he's American, but super-conservative. Thinks that Las Vegas in lights is sleazy. So I . . . sleazed it up for him."

"In my dress?"

"Girls, girls, girls!" Danny Dove's expressive eyebrows were chinning themselves on his curly blond hairline as he stared their way. "Chatting is for dressing rooms; working our buns off is for rehearsals, and silence is golden. Keep it that way or it'll be thirty lashes with a wet eyelash and, my dears, the eyelashes you little hoofers wear come long enough to sting!"

The others giggled while Darcy and Trish tapped in silence for a while. But three minutes later they labored shoulder-to-shoulder again.

"So you wasted my dress on a professor," Trish lamented. "I bet he didn't even notice; I bet all you got out of it was an 'A' for effrontery."

Darcy shrugged and tapped her way down the line

turning rapid circles, doing what Danny Dove had recommended, concentrating.

"Okay, boys and girls. Time for a break—for *moi!* I can't stand watching you raggamuffins much longer. Twenty minutes and then we all pitter-patter our hearts out."

Exhausted dancers sank to the stage floor where they stood, or sat on the stage apron, their silver tap shoes dangling glamorously below lumpy rolls of wool leg warmers. Some slid slowly recumbent against the proscenium arch; others collapsed in clumps behind the scenery to take furtive drags on community cigarettes.

Darcy stayed center-stage, staring at the vast, empty, dark theatrical house, trying to imagine where Steven had sat when he'd attended the revue the night before. The night before . . . IT . . . happened. He probably hadn't had the savvy to tip the maitre d' for a good seat, she considered wistfully, her imagination assigning him a spot somewhere well beyond the side sight lines at the very summit of the raked seating area.

"So." Trish threw herself down beside Darcy. "Did it work?"

"I thought you were mad because I took your dress."

"I've decided I'm more curious than furious, honey. Well, did it work?"

"Too well," Darcy admitted. "He thinks I'm the exact opposite of myself."

"Hmmmm. . . ." Trish leaned back to eye Darcy critically. "For once you must have made a good impression on a guy. Keep it up." Trish patted Darcy's knee, then pushed off it as she rose to the atunal accompaniment of groans before moving away.

Darcy straddled her long legs wide for some slow stretching exercises, drying a necklace of beaded sweat with the sleeve of her leotard. Some glamorous life, she thought, glancing to the imaginary man watching in the farthest seat. Maybe you're right, Stevenson Eliot Austen. Maybe all this is unnatural.

Danny Dove dismissed the weekly brush-up rehearsal at four that afternoon, bawling threats of calling another before the week was out. Instead of milling outside the stage door with the gang, Darcy headed in an opposite, unusual direction—through the lobby of the Crystal Phoenix.

Like all who work behind the scenes of a great enterprise—be it cruise ship or Broadway hit or Las Vegas hotel—Darcy seldom saw the Crystal Phoenix's public areas, taking their existence for granted.

Now she lolled past busy craps and twenty-one tables, basking under endless shimmering strings of crystal.

The hotel decor had managed to marry elegance to flamboyance and send them on a honeymoon. Even in the casino, where clinking coins, chips and cocktail glasses drowned out even the high excited whines of the winners (losers invariably kept quiet), Darcy could hear the natural chime of falling water. She could see the light-filled bubbles of the hotel's lounge and restaurant areas strung around the vast inner cave of eternal darkness where money was lost and won and lost again.

She meandered through this Crystal Promenade, rinsed by the rushing water sandwiched between the glass panels that formed its roof. Her feet trod large varnished flagstones inset into the hotel floor with deceptively casual precision. In the foaming whirlpools, couples cavorted unselfconsciously. In nearby still ponds the water dimpled around imported greenery and small man-made waterfalls announced their headlong choreographed presence around the next corner.

A narrow neck of shops led to the hotel's rear courtyard and pool, and beyond it Darcy found the perpetually shaded peace of the fish pond. A slight, nondescript man was standing there, wearing over his pants the raucous, short-sleeved holiday shirt beloved of tourists and certain low-brow, high-flash habituees of gaming establishments. He greeted her with a couplet.

"It looks like the gams of Darcy the Dancer have ambled poolside in search of an answer."

"An answer to what, Nostradamus?"

The wizened man shrugged, pulling a half-smoked stogie from his brilliantly floral shirt pocket.

"My eyes could be lying and my instincts double-crossed. All I can say is, you look like you're lost."

"Hey, the Crystal Phoenix is my home, for Pete's sake!" Darcy sat on the small retaining wall to study the glinting fish that glanced past. "I'm not lost . . . I'm pensive. Have you ever done something that was exactly what you wanted to do, only—it wasn't?"

Nostradamus's leathery face cracked like the desert floor in a drought as he smiled and pulled the snap brim of his straw fedora into a jaunty, Jimmy Durante angle.

"You ask if I've ever lost my heart to regret? Darcy, honey, it happens every time I bet."

"But you're a bookie. You're supposed to win and lose and roll with the dice." Darcy trailed a languid hand in the water. Goldfish churned into bright butter around it, expecting food. When she looked up, Nostradamus had melted into the mob of stripped and greased hotel guests arrayed beneath the palms to soak up the pool's reflected sunlight.

The reason for Nostradamus' sudden exit came pushing through the tinted glass doors, his cream silk-and-wool-blend jacket flapping over an open-necked ivory silk shirt.

"You seen Nostradamus anywhere?" Nicky demanded abruptly, the gold medal of St. Jude at his neck echoing the glint in his eye.

"Yes, but he's gone."

"Damn!" Nicky's tanned fists pushed back the jacket to prop themselves on his hips as he unsuccessfully studied the poolside population.

"Win a bet?" Darcy asked sympathetically.

"No, but I wanted some dope on someone who did. That little guy can melt away like whipped butter when he wants to. Hey, how come you're moping by Sing's pond?"

"I'm not moping! I'm beat from five hours on my feet with Danny Dove."

"Okay, but don't trail your tootsies in Sing's private cooler there. Those fish are finned treasures to him." Nicky looked at her a moment longer, then plunged. "Van and I were just saying, we three ought to get together for dinner or something. This hotel game gets hectic, but we don't want to forget old friends."

"Sure," Darcy said. "But I'm frantic myself between the show and classes."

Nicky's fingers snapped remembrance. "That's right. You're toting books on the university campus these days, too. How's it going?"

"Dandy. Just dandy," she said sardonically.

"Good. Glad to hear it. I gotta admire you for going back to get a degree. What're you studying anyway?"

"English."

Nicky's lean face tautened in bemusement. "English. Well, why not? We all gotta speak it, so to speak, even Nostradamus. Where is that weasel—?"

Darcy stood, resting her slender hands on Nicky's shoulders until he stopped fidgeting and looked her in the eye. He was about her height and exactly her age, but she often wore high heels and always thought of him as her little brother.

"Nicky, you're a swell fellah and all, but don't try to encourage people in noble causes for their own good. It's not your style."

He relaxed suddenly and winked, his quick hands squeezing her arms. "You're okay, Darce, even if you do learn to challenge Nostradamus to rhyming duels at twenty paces or something. Don't let anyone stop you at what you think you should do. That's the only advice I've got a right to give, 'cause I followed it and look at me now"—Nicky's arms swung as wide as Vic Damone's on a high note—"infamous hotelier and all-round nice guy who has the smartest wife with the best legs in Vegas."

Nicky paused halfway through the glass doors as second thoughts caught up with him.

"Uh, your legs are pretty good, too, professionally speaking." His hand curled back and forth in a gesture more easily understood than translated. "Not bad." Nicky nodded authoritatively. "You'll do okay."

Sirene leaned thoughtfully against her cluttered dressing table edge. Legs as long as ladders stretched into the small room's center, and were delicately crossed at the ankles.

Standing at her feet, quite literally, was a man in a dark green suit that looked like it had been on him longer than his chronic five-o'clock shadow. It bagged where he sagged. A tongue of salmon pink tie protruded from a shapeless suitcoat pocket. The shade almost precisely matched the color of his eyes, which were not so much bloodshot as blood-poached.

"I'm on a roll, Sirene," he was saying. "Come on, what've you got better to do after the show than hit the craps tables? They'll be gathering around the green-felt riverbank when I roll, baby. Whada ya say?"

Professor Stevenson Eliot Austen's piercing gray eyes confronted his class through his lenses as he looked up from the papers in his hand. Once again, Darcy McGill's work was on the critiquing block. He pushed his glasses lower on the bridge of his nose. His judgment was going AWOL. He didn't *want* to find out if Sirene would go out with the low-life gambler. He didn't want to think of Sirene living the flashy life of a chorus queen when all he could see was her languorous length in his arms. And when he glimpsed Darcy's clean-scrubbed face at the back of the classroom, he couldn't bear to think of Sirene, and what had happened seven days before, at all.

"It goes on," he interrupted the narrative, "in like vein. I doubt we need to read at length. You all are familiar with Miss McGill's Las Vegas fables."

The author in question slouched in a rear seat as usual. Steven had seen her enter and had tried to pretend that he had not, as he had done every other day this week, which was how often the creative writing class met—Monday, Wednesday, and today, Friday.

A hand in the front row rose tentatively.

"Yes, Mrs. Warren, you had a question or comment?"

"Question," chirped the woman, who was attending college on the empty-nest plan. "What happens? Does Sirene go out with the compulsive gambler? And isn't the sheik's son due back from Abba Dhabba any day now?"

Steven winced. He'd forgotten, yet *another* suitor of Sirene's. He managed to quirk a smile toward the top row. "There, you see, Miss McGill? The first reward granted the beginning writer—an avid reader. If you like, class, Miss McGill can copy her assignments before class and distribute installments."

To his chagrin, heads nodded eagerly across the rows—except the shiny brown head he could barely see. He had perched, as usual, on the edge of his desk while he read. He leaned, Tower-of-Pisa-style, to his right but found his quarry hidden by the naturally curly mane of "Spider" Phlugg, a student by day and electric-bongo player by night.

Casually shifting his books, Steven leaned left. But no matter how he positioned himself, Darcy McGill was always obscured from his view. He began to think it deliberate, and, miffed, leaned further. Balance lost the bet. Only the quick planting of a foot saved him from taking an embarrassing fall in front of his class.

Steven glowered behind the severe black frames of his glasses. "Class is over, but Miss McGill can stay for a private critique," he announced firmly.

By twos and threes, they left, fifteen ardent souls determined to master English prose style. One stayed behind, exactly where she was.

Steven purposefully climbed the stairs to her seat and sat on the adjacent desk. He cast the most recent of the adventures of Miss Sirene McGill to the other desktop.

"You're sticking with your Sirene stories."

"Yes." She didn't look up. "I like them."

"Well, you have company. So, apparently, does the class."

"Not you?" She glanced up, one quick clean look from doe-shy hazel eyes.

92

"Does it matter? I'm only the instructor," he jested.

"Yes," she said breathily, as if speaking just before she had found the air for it. "You are the instructor."

He studied her. Where Sirene was bare and polished by all the art the stage could assemble, her sister was plain, a matte finish of washed denim, soft-woven sweaters, and unglossed facial features. Only her hair and eyes shone, natural as rainwater.

He sighed. "Does your sister know how thoroughly you embellish her life?"

"Oh, I don't embellish it. Not much, anyway."

"She really has all these men coming around?"

A rapid flash of eye contact darted from under her drawn curtains of hair. "All these men, from all walks of life, even—"

"Yes?" He was leaning forward, *Norton's Anthology of English Literature* in his hand bracing him on the table.

"—even doctors and lawyers. No Indian chiefs—yet."

"I'm relieved to hear it. But surely she doesn't, er, go out with all those men?"

"I think you mean . . ." Her voice sank to a whisper. "Go to bed with."

He stood. "I am perfectly capable of saying what I mean. I am not inquiring into your sister's morals, Miss McGill. That is none of my business and, I would imagine, none of yours. It's simply that since you admit she's a real person—"

"Oh, she is! Even showgirls are real persons."

He squinted at her downcast features, detecting irony or some other savage twist behind the innocent face value of her words.

"You know what I mean, Miss McGill," he finally said. "When you write about a real person, you invade his or her privacy. How would you like it if I took you for the heroine of my short fiction, and speculated on your social life?"

"I'd say you'd have a dull story." Her eyes were twinkling up at him, but he found her self-deprecating humor irritating.

"There! That's it. There you go putting yourself down again! Your sister Sirene may lead a more glamorous life than you do, she's an attractive, vital woman—"

"How do you know?"

He stared into the eyes that now had no difficulty meeting his. "Why, uh—I'm assuming, naturally, that she resembles you. She is your twin, after all. And then, all these . . . men . . . seem endlessly attracted to her—in your stories."

Darcy McGill shrugged. "Oh, Professor Austen. Men are always attracted to showgirls, not mousy little scholars; it goes with the territory. You get used to it."

One of her phrases sounded familiar, but this conversation gave Steven no heart to search for a literary source. He stuck to the point. "You mean *you* get used to Sirene getting all the attention, don't you?"

"Are you trying to psychoanalyze me, Professor?"

He backed off. "No. Of course not. That doesn't go with the territory. I wonder, though. What is your occupation? Off-campus, that is."

Her long forefinger balanced on the blond desktop on a short pale nail that traced a fleeting pattern.

"I, ah, work for a hotel. Behind the scenes. You'd be amazed how many people work behind the scenes."

"Quite a little Cinderella, aren't you? Evading the spotlight?"

She looked up from the half-truth she half-hoped he would challenge. His head was cocked in an attitude of

shouldertop. The sensation was exquisite.

They swayed together, lips almost touching, Darcy's face tilted to avoid his glasses. Why hadn't Sirene removed them long before this if she was such a vamp?

"You're sure?" Darcy asked. Not Sirene, but Darcy asked, who wanted to be wanted for being Darcy. "You're sure you don't want to . . . Friday night again?"

"No!" He released her so quickly she nearly fell over.

Steven already had wheeled to face the mantel. His fist, white-knuckled, pounded soft denial on the huge weather-cracked timber. When he opened it, the Crystal Phoenix matchbook lay on his palm.

"I'll start a fire." He bent quickly to the grate, forcing her to step back from the fireplace. "Nights get cold on the desert, even in the fall."

"Yes." Her frozen tone of voice alone ratified his comment.

By the time the Crystal Phoenix's efficient matches had coaxed a fringe of flame around the top log, Darcy's internal fires were firmly banked.

Steven rose and ran a hand through the thick hair at his temple. He glanced very quickly at her dress. "Do you need a sweater? I have one—"

She shook her head no.

He strode, emitting nervous energy, behind the couch and took up a lecturer's position, his hands curling into the gaily dyed wool as into a podium rim. "Maybe this throw would make a shawl."

"I'm fine," she said. "Plenty warm. What did you want to tell me, then?"

"Only that—" He cleared his throat as he did when opening a class. One hand swept to indicate the mutedly colorful book spines blooming on every wall around him

113

like gilt-stamped wallpaper. "Only that there's a whole world outside the dressing room of a Las Vegas revue. I don't know how you and Darcy can be so different."

"We're sisters, not soul mates," Sirene retorted.

He leaned intently over the sofa back, his strong hands splayed on the now-rumpled blanket. Professor Stevenson Eliot Austen had always been a most passionate teacher.

"What do you read?" he demanded.

Sirene stepped forward uncertainly as the swelling flames heaved toward the chimney behind her, their sudden heat tinging her already rouged cheeks with genuine warmth.

"Darcy's stories," she began, as if hoping for approval.

"Good, good."

"And the Chamber of Commerce *Visitors' Guide to Las Vegas*."

He nodded, not encouraged but urging her on.

Sirene took fire. "The . . . the *TV Guide*! And, and sometimes, when she's not looking, Darcy's diary. And—I bought a book at the grocery store the other day—*Your New Millennium Horoscope*! Say, what's your sign? I'm a Gemini."

"Well, you're certainly no Virgo," he snapped, crestfallen.

"Huh? Of course not; I told you—my sign's Gemini. What's your sign? Tell me!"

"I don't know," Steven answered irritatedly, pacing with his hands in his pockets while he searched for a new approach.

"You don't know your own horoscope sign?" Deep shock colored Sirene's tones. "How old are you, anyway?"

"Thirty-two, and I've lived quite nicely that long without knowing my sign."

"That's hard to believe, that a person could live that long

without knowing something as basic as that."

"Maybe it's basic in your circles, but not mine. Look here, Sirene." He pounced on the mangled blanket again, leaning over the sofa top as a new idea struck him. "You've heard of Sherlock Holmes, haven't you?"

"Sure." A smile stretched her glossy crimson lips. "You kinda dress like him in those tweedy jackets. And he smokes a pipe, too. I've seen all those 2 A.M. reruns with Razzle Bathbone."

Steven clapped a hand to his forehead and shut his eyes.

"That's . . . encouraging. Well, Sherlock Holmes, even though he was the greatest detective in the world, didn't know that the earth turned around the sun! And when Dr. Watson showed astonishment that he didn't, Holmes said it wasn't important to his life—what revolved around what out there. That's like me. I don't care what sign I was born under, I only care what I can make of myself where I am now, do you see?"

Sirene nodded seriously, her long lashes casting spiky shadows on her rosy cheeks. "That's a lovely story, but . . . does it?"

"Does it what?"

"You know"—her forefinger pointed to the ceiling and made a coy rotation—"revolve around us, or do we revolve around it?"

He sighed explosively as his hands slapped against his thighs. "I guess it doesn't matter that much at that. Sirene, come here," he added sternly.

"I thought we weren't—"

"We're not. We're going to talk. That's all. Talk. You know, we move our lips and words come out."

"You're sure you're not proposing something else in the lip department? You're awfully deep, Doc. Sometimes I'm not sure you mean what you say."

His hand extended over the brown leather couch between them and then he guided her around it to his side as he turned to indicate the book-thick shelves.

"Do you know how many books there are in this room?" She shook her head. "Well, I don't either, but it's a lot; and they're on all sorts of subjects—fiction, history, language."

He guided her to one solid wall of tomes. The firelight across the room picked out the winking gleam of their golden titles in letters as vivid as those on Las Vegas's neon signs. Steven pulled out one butter-soft leather-bound book, its pages edged in gold. His palm repeatedly smoothed the surface in a gesture that made Darcy swallow as he placed the book softly in her hands.

"This one's over a hundred years old. A collection of poems by Shelley, who died at thirty. This book has outlived him by generations. There are stories in all these books, Sirene. Look at them, handle them. Give them a chance."

"You sound like my agent hustling me to producers for a job," Sirene said wryly. But she took the book, flipping the gilt-edged pages until their golden glimmer fanned her face. "I get enough poe-try from Nostradamus." She handed it back.

"Nostradamus? Where'd you get that name? Nostradamus was a famous sixteenth-century French astrologer! His rhymed prophecies astound people even today. Especially with the Millennium almost on us." Steven looked genuinely hopeful. "Perhaps . . . the humble horoscope *is* your path to knowledge, after all."

She shrugged, sending the magenta silk dipping again. His anxious fingers caught it, then patted it back into proper position.

"Last I knew," Sirene mused, "Nostradamus was this flaky bookie on the Strip, a sweet old guy, only he talks like something out of *Mother Goose*, you know?"

Steven stared at her, but Sirene whirled gracefully to confront the bookcases, the side slit of her skirt revealing a flash of white thigh. She ran her nails over the assembled spines, finally pouncing upon one title.

"*Lady Chatterly's Lover.* Now that one I've heard about." The long red-lacquered nails were paging through the unexpurgated edition.

"That's . . . uh, that's literature."

Sirene's dubious eyes darted up from the pages.

"Really. Literature, so help me God," he said.

"Hmmm." Sirene's eyes, the lashes lowered so they lay on her cheeks like ebony fringe, read. "This looks like pretty hot literature to me, Professor, all that white flesh and horizontal recreation."

He snatched back the book. "It's literature, I tell you! It may deal with the sensuous side of life, but profoundly. It's nothing like those tawdry books one finds on the supermarket racks."

"Hey." Sirene's hands posed Mae-West-style on her hips, pinching in the loose lines of the silk dress against the streamlined structure beneath. "I read a few of those. How do you know what's in 'em, Professor? Aren't you judging a book by its cover? How do you know that what they're about isn't a heck of a lot more real to people today than all these old books that've been studied to death by people who don't remember—or maybe never knew—anything about what's what."

"Like . . . ?"

"Like . . ." Sirene's flirtatious tongue reglossed her already gleaming red lips. "Like sex and love and all that stuff in *Lady Chatterly's Lover.* I may not be a brain, but I know a thing or two about that."

He stared at her as he slipped the Lawrence novel back into its slot between Durrell and W. H. Auden. "I bet you do."

"Now this," Sirene went on boldly. "I bet this is a real good book. Read me something out of that."

He glanced at the title. *Love Lyrics.*

"This is seventeenth-century poetry, Sirene. Cavalier lyrics. I'm not sure—"

"I am." She leaned back against the shelves, her face tilted at the ceiling. "I bet that book's got the right stuff. Read me some, Steven. Convert me," she challenged, with a direct glance he couldn't quite meet.

So he looked down, flipped open a page, and began reading aloud. His voice dropped to the deep, intense range in which he sought to convey the beauty of the written word to his students.

" 'Whenas in silks my Julia goes'—he glanced across the shimmering azalea-bright fabric sheathing his listener— " 'Then, then, methinks, how sweetly flows/That liquifaction of her clothes.' "

Sirene's inch-long lashes snapped open. "What's 'liquifaction'?"

"An archaic word . . . not used anymore. The poet is attempting to convey how the silk moves around his mistress's body, how it ebbs and flows like water. Liquid."

"Oh." Moving, Sirene sent her own silks into a ripple of indiscretion that first transfixed, then repelled, Steven's gaze.

"That poem doesn't say much," he said quickly, his voice oddly choked. The academic tone revived. "Ah, here's another by Herbert on the similar subject: 'A sweet disorder in the dress/Kindles in clothes a wantonness. A lawn about the shoulders thrown into a fine distraction—' "

"She's wearing grass on her neck?"

"No, no." Steven smiled benignly. " 'Lawn' was a fine-woven fabric. Here the poet pays tribute to a lack of artifice in a woman, which is far more enticing than perfection. The 'lawn about the shoulders thrown' could be your dress."

His fingers flirted across Sirene's shifting neckline in his eagerness to clarify seventeenth-century meaning, inadvertently pushing it completely off her shoulder before referring again to the text.

"Her clothing has slipped, which puts the lover 'into a fine distraction.' It . . . um, intrigues him more than seeing you . . . her . . . half-undressed in any spotlight in Las Vegas, you see? It distracts his eye from whatever he was doing"—he demonstrated by looking from open book to undraped shoulder—"this very unexpected . . . glimpse . . . of soft revealed flesh." His voice lowered as his eyes caressed what his words had described. "That's what—nobody—appreciates today. The finesse of the half-spoken word, the partially revealed form."

"Ooooh!" Sirene caught her shoulders in a shivery self-embrace, thrusting the bared one into high relief. "You give me goosebumps when you talk like that, Professor. That poet-guy may be dead and buried, but he sure knew what he was talking about. This is a lot better than Nostradamus' jingles. Read me some more."

His eyes were darting desperately about the page even as he pushed his glasses more firmly into place.

" 'Next, when I cast mine eyes, and see/That brave vibration, each way free,/O, how that glittering taketh me!' "

That Julia chick sounds like she can *move*," Sirene said admiringly. "Was she a hoofer, too?"

He clapped the book shut. "No. She was just a mistress. Sirene—"

"Yes?" Darcy leaned against the books, feeling the leather-bound spirits of Shelley and Byron, of Herbert and Lovelace, of the Brontës and Jane Austen, seeping from their buttressing spines into hers. Her eyes were closed.

"Sirene. I'm trying to be reasonable about this." Steven's voice was torn with tension, a blend of confusion and desire.

She opened her eyes. He had forgotten the books and was reading her now—her face, her body, her thoughts. Lord, she hoped he wasn't reading her thoughts!

"You can't be reasonable about this, Steven. Not even a little bit."

"I don't want to hurt anyone. You. Me. Darcy."

"Darcy's a big girl," she whispered. "She might surprise you."

"Poor little Darcy." He spoke with bitter self-reproach as he turned his face away. "I tell her to stop writing about her sister Sirene, and here I am, aching to make love to her."

"You are? Really?"

His sweeping self-contempt kept him from noticing the naive pleasure of her response. He continued berating himself.

"It's not fair to Darcy, or to you! But there's something about you. It's a purely carnal attraction, I'm afraid. We have nothing in common—nothing!" He paced in front of her like a man leashed by the magnetic pull of her body.

"We have Darcy," she said quietly.

He stopped and stared at her again, as if expecting her to transform into a more intellectually palatable form.

"I'm very fond of Darcy," he said in some distress. "I respect her talent, her intelligence. I wouldn't want to do anything to hurt her."

"Why do you think making love to me would hurt

Darcy? You don't think *she's*—"

Whatever Sirene had been about to say, Steven stopped it with the sudden passionate muffling of his mouth on hers. "No!" he answered as he broke the kiss, as much distracted as ever. "Not Darcy. Nothing like that. The idea of our deception, though. . . ."

"She might love it," Sirene coaxed reasonably. "A new chapter in her continuing story."

"Oh, God," he said, horrified.

Sirene smiled and reached up to pull off his glasses. "You're not reading anymore, sweet. You don't need these. I'm close enough so you can see me perfectly."

His head dropped chestward in defeat. "Heaven help me."

"Heaven helps those who help themselves. I heard that somewhere once," Sirene cooed confidently. She glimmered, sparkled, scintillated up at him. "So . . . help yourself," she invited.

With a groan of defeat, Stevenson Eliot Austen took Sirene Darcy McGill into his arms and kissed her with more passion than had been poured onto a page since the days of the long-dead and dusty Cavalier poets.

Behind their entwined forms, Cavalier poets and lady novelists lost their upright positions and lurched into a coeducational slide from which it was possible that modern literature would never recover.

♥ Chapter Ten ♥

Love Lyrics lay open-face down on the floor—a position that did irretrievable insult to its venerable, gold-stamped spine.

Two entire shelves of books sagged drunkenly against one another—classics allowed to play slovens, untidied and unattended.

The bright plaid blanket lay heaped behind the large brown leather bulk of the Chesterfield sofa. Not far from it reclined an expensively tailored herringbone tweed sportcoat, abandoned in an uncannily lifelike position, so it looked as if its occupant had been sucked out of it by some scaly denizen of a three-A.M. television monster movie.

Atop it rested the graceful, empty superstructure of a single high-heeled bronze sandal.

Beyond the horizon of the Chesterfield, rampant firelight leaped up the chimney's charred throat and the regular beat of a soft-rock station thrummed from the stereo receiver alongside the fireplace.

A leg, white and bare, suddenly rose periscope-stiff above the sofa top. The ankle rotated expertly, the toes pointed impressively and in a moment the mate to the abandoned sandal dangled half-off the instep. One kick of well-articulated calf muscles sent the shoe plummeting down to join its mate on the jacket, albeit in a most disorganized fashion.

Sirene's slightly disheveled topknot peeped over the leather a moment later, rising as the leg disappeared. She gravely surveyed the positioning of her discard.

Steven's face surfaced a second later.

122

of practicing ballet when she was growing up—and then the actual growing up process itself. Imagine being a girl and five-feet-eight at thirteen! Who would ask you to dance at parties—Dr. J? And Sirene just kept growing and growing. Oh, it's okay for ballerinas to be a little tall, but nearly six feet? And living in Las Vegas, where the most widely recognized form of dance means taking off most of your clothes and parading in front of hordes of lascivious men."

" 'Lascivious.' Yes, they are that," he interjected guiltily. "You mean that her forward manner—the manner that you portray so masterfully in your stories, that is—is all a front?"

Darcy sighed. "Now that you mention 'front' you must realize that Sirene was cursed with a good figure, however elongated. Too much 'front' for the ballet stage; she'd fall over. There was only one thing left for a girl who loved to dance and liked to eat—the life of the Las Vegas showgirl," Darcy declaimed melodramatically.

"Think how awful it is to have men always ogling your body; I mean, you're finally leading a glamorous life, and all they want is surface, surface, surface. All they want"— Darcy leaned confidently closer and lowered her voice "—is to *sleep* with you."

"No!" The shock in his voice rang terribly true. "Perhaps not *all* men?"

"All men." Darcy shook her head sadly. "They're so shallow. They don't care what you think, what your aspirations are. They're all alike." She slipped him a sideways glance as numbing as a mickey. "Of course, I wouldn't be so frank if I didn't know that you're different, Professor, that you would understand, being sensitive to words and people and relationships."

" 'Relationships.' Yes, that's a big part of writing, isn't

it?" He had gone from mellow to limp. "Sometimes I think I hardly understand anything at all."

His eyes shifted from the distance to Darcy's.

"What about you?" he asked. "You were her twin, after all. What was growing up like for you?"

She shrugged. "The same in some ways, only I spent all my time reading instead of doing pliés. Pliés," she explained. "You know, you stand like a pigeon and pump up and down with your knees. It's one of the basics of ballet."

"You've lost me." His fingers tapped on the bench's top rail. "I guess I don't know much about anything, except books."

Darcy noticed with surprise that his arm lay casually on the bench behind her. She felt a vague qualm at having misled him down yet another garden path well planted with half-truths.

"Me too," she agreed bitterly.

"Books are as good a place as any to hide, Darcy," he said softly, his gaze turning suddenly shrewd. "That, I do know a bit about. So when Sirene emerged from her cocoon to spread her terpsichorean wings, you were left in the audience to watch, is that it?"

"In a way. Some of us have to shine, and some of us have to watch."

"Are you shy?" he asked suddenly.

"About . . . some things. Like—my writing."

"And I jumped all over it." His fingers lifted from the bench to brush vaguely at her loosened hair. "Poor Darcy—caught between the devil and the deep blue sea."

"Who's the devil?" she asked breathlessly.

"Me, I suppose. And Sirene's the deep blue sea." His voice had softened betrayingly on the last words. Darcy felt a sharp spasm of jealousy. She did envy Sirene—now. She had manufactured her own rival.

"Darcy." Steven easily read the misery in her eyes. "You're a great survivor, I can tell. You've been such a good sport about my sniping at your stories, about Sirene getting the spotlight. Let's start over, you and I. I'd like to be your friend."

"Sure," Darcy said, standing. "A good sport can always use a friend. Look, I gotta run. Sorry."

And she did. She ran away, leaving Professor Austen late for his class and sitting surprised on a campus bench. She ran all the way to the parking lot behind the Humanities Building to her car, then flung her books and papers any which way onto the passenger seat.

The Nova burped into gear when she started it and whipped her through the post-five P.M. rush-hour traffic along Tropicana. She got to the Crystal Phoenix just in time to charge through the stage door, wave at Jake, run to the dressing room, pat Louie on his pillow, and crash-land in front of the mirror to paint Sirene back on her face.

"Hey, Darce, you're late and quiet tonight," Midge noted, bending to straighten the seams on her leggy lattice-work of fishnet hose. "Where's the house hooligan we know and love?"

"Out to lunch." Darcy ripped off an eyelash that had glued itself askew and tried again.

Beautifully drawn eyebrows lifted in concert while the three queens silently consulted each other.

"Things a little tough with classes and work and all?" Jo asked. "Are you carrying too big a load?"

"Yeah. Things are a little tough."

The tension in Darcy's shoulders loosened as she roughly pinned up her hair. What was she worrying about? All she had to do was whistle and Steven would come running to Sirene, whether he understood the urge or not.

"I'm sorry, kids," she apologized. "I'm a little tired, that's all."

"Well, if that professor is working you too hard, you just tell him to go jump in Lake Mead," Trish advised. "No grade is worth wearing yourself down to a nub for."

Darcy remained silent.

"Are you playing hide-and-seek with that guy, is that it?" Trish went on. "Is that why you had us not use your name in front of him? What's going on?"

"Nothing that's any of your business," Darcy answered quickly. "If I fall down the lucite staircase in the Four Queens number you'll have reason to wonder if I'm losing my rhinestones. Until then, my feet are firmly on the ground."

She planted her silver tap shoes aggressively on the concrete and stared at her friends one by one until their mascara-coated lashes lowered and she was no longer the center of attention.

Only the black cat named Midnight Louie kept watching at her from his statuesque position on the red pillow atop her dressing table. He stared skeptically for a good thirty seconds while Darcy defiantly matched his gaze, then let his green eyes wink out in bored turn. He yawned elaborately and Darcy inwardly agreed; this double life she led was beginning to be a bore.

Had Danny Dove observed Darcy sleepwalking her way through twenty-four costume changes involving some eight hundred pounds of high-carat rhinestones, he would have blanched to his white kid soft shoes. Luckily, Danny Dove was in Majorca mounting a transvestite revue.

Usually the Royal Suite of Cards Revue's opening number with its special effects miming a Technicolor sun-

144

rise on the rear scrim left Darcy cornily breathless.

Tonight the sherbet-luscious lighting effects melted into each other like sun-baked M & M's.

Sunrise, sunset, Darcy sang sourly to herself as she paraded—along with thirty sister hoofers—in the pearl-draped, peach ostrich-feather ensemble that represented a ray of dawn sunshine. Like a curtain, life rose and fell with a certain predictability, she mused to the music. Darcy was definitely in a down cycle, but she never missed a step of her routine. Like her infamous sister, Sirene, she was a pro.

The western sky bled watercolors through the clouds and down over the shrouded mountaintops. Sun-loving lizards skittered into rockside shelter. Gentle desert Rosy Boas basked in the setting sun's last rays as they slithered on their nocturnal grocery shopping expeditions along with scaled cousins of the rattlesnake clan.

Creosote bushes rustled with the stirrings of nocturnal mice and kangaroo rats. Nightwinged birds of prey slowly scoured the darkening sky.

A man on horseback was not a common sight in this grandly brutal landscape, but neither was it unexpected.

Quaker waited quietly, as if knowing his noble profile stood etched against the pale evening clouds like a Remington bronze. Steven sat the heavily tooled Western saddle as stoically. He rode as he followed all his pursuits—privately, for his own enjoyment, and better than anyone would suspect.

Tonight's sunset unfurled a particularly ravishing assortment of shade and substance; clouds like streaming banners dyed a bloody death in the West.

Steven's eyes, unfocused through lenses, saw in their subtly melding shapes the glare of red-gelled spotlights and the soft, feathery drift of ostrich plumes. Venus, rising behind him in the east, shone like the solar system's largest rhinestone.

Steven pulled the reins over Quaker's neck. The horse leaned into the motion as liquidly as if it had invented the notion of turning just then. Soon its iron-cloven hooves were cantering smartly through the soft surface sand, thumping onto the hard-packed rock below.

Home before dark, Steven internally urged the horse. He felt the sunset dwindling to a copper wire of light narrow as a garrote at his back, felt the dangerous desert dark sliding over him like a lizard's inner eyelid.

But Quaker liked a run and knew the way. Familiar silhouettes of Joshua trees flashed by, their cactus arms flexed into right angles as inflexible as any traffic cop's. Steven saw the dark clump that was his acreage swelling ahead and pulled Quaker to a trot.

He walked the animal into the corral and rubbed him down thoroughly in the small shed that served as a stable. Quaker was tough; neither desert sun nor nighttime chill would keep him from his appointed equine role. He nickered good-night as Steven walked up to the house. Visions of the raucous, bawdy world Sirene inhabited seared Steven's mind despite the tranquilizer of natural beauty.

Inside, he threw off his windbreaker and left it over a kitchen chairback, a break in an otherwise compulsively neat routine. He donned his glasses to prowl the bookcases, purportedly looking for something to read. He ended up straightening the toppled volumes, then running his fingers along their imprinted spines and over their leather-scented bindings.

Once he pulled out a book and opened it, reading at random. It was D. H. Lawrence. "This is literature," he remembered saying. He believed it then and did now. His eyes hovered over one of the unsurpassably sensuous passages—not scandalous stuff by today's standards but frankly sensual. Maybe that was literature, too.

Steven cast himself from room to room in the small house, searching for the simple satisfying pursuits that he'd always found to distract him in an evening. He prided himself on being self-sufficient. Now that self seemed fragmented, torn in two, maybe three, directions.

It longed for city lights and wicked ways; it hungered for quiet walks and sensible talks, for a reliable mind and eyes as endlessly soft as dusk when the light goes from hazel to night's brunette beauty.

Brunette Beauty. His fingers flipped open the Cavalier poets to that very verse, then snapped it shut again. Such sentiments were three hundred years behind the times. Give him a liberated woman—with sex appeal.

In his bedroom, Steven studied the cocoa down comforter, undented by any presence since morning. The bedside digital clock told him it was too early to retire; too late to look for a distraction outside the house.

The spare bedroom served as an office. Steven drew the plastic cover off the royal blue IBM Selectric and ran his fingertips over the keys. When he sat down at it, as he had not done in months, he pulled out a drawer and extracted the entombed corpses of his fiction writing. White and dry they were, these pieces of his past; they rustled like dead leaves, each tucked into its own shroud of clear-plastic folder, each neatly prepared for interment by the local professional typist.

He scanned a few pages and tossed the papers back into the drawer. Literary fiction. Academic exercises, dry as lizard dust. Stories of failed faculty wives and arid intellectual lives. He saw why he had stopped. "Epiphanies" in checkout lines, dissections of infidelity among the chronically unfaithful.

Slowly, his mind churning with mixed images of a peacock-feathered woman and calm, insightful eyes, Steven pulled a fresh white page off his nearby stack of twenty-pound bond. He glanced at the brand on the carton. Neenah Bond. His fingers, in the sparring way of most male typists, punched in the byline—Ned Bond.

He sat up straighter and pulled his chair closer to the desk. Light poured its honey down on the platen from the amber-glassed banker's lamp at his right hand. The letters tapped onto the page, bold, extravagant words unrolling with their own impudent purpose and style.

He wrote of the desert and night and Las Vegas, shimmering like a devilish oasis of electricity in the dark. He invented mean streets and meaner men who walked them, trailing danger. He became part Chandler and Lawrence and Cornell Wollrich. Mystery smoked from the barrel of his prose as he pumped word after word onto the pages; death and love and sex and Sirene's earthy "all that stuff" entwined in a murky, entertaining dance as the silver metal ball spun, stringing letters like black pearls across the white page.

The typewriter keys chattered rhythmically into the night, tap dancing in some preordained, unforeseen routine. Steven felt he was in two places at once, alone and not alone, uncertain and sure. Excitement boiled in him—partly because Sirene wasn't here and he was thinking of her, partly because he was alone and oblivious to her for once.

Neither state seemed like the answer, but he kept on writing.

Darcy bent over to unbuckle the red satin T-strap pumps

from her Red-Queen costume.

"I'm beat," Midge said behind her, echoing her thoughts. "You better head straight home and hit the sack," she advised in her dorm-mother voice.

"Sure." Darcy sat up with a gravity-reddened face. "I haven't got anything on tonight but makeup."

"I was hoping," Trish hinted shamelessly, "that your cute professor might show up again."

"No such luck." Darcy stood to jump herself into her jeans.

The other women stopped their own re-dressing to watch her with open eyes and minds. Aware of their vigilance, Darcy pulled on a loose sweatshirt over her glitter-dusted Lily of France bra, then grabbed her purse and tote bag from under her chair.

"I've got to run if I'm going to catch up on sleep. 'Night, all," she threw to them as a parting bone.

She spurted down the corridor, calling out cheery goodnights to everyone she passed. Jake at his desk got a hand wave and a wink as Darcy eeled through the door leading to the casino.

From overlit one-A.M. cool-down, Darcy plunged into dimly lit early-morning aerobic mania in the gambling area. Grown men exhorted dice to lay right for them as onlookers cheered and groaned. Diamond-draped women dressed gloriously enough to make Nancy Reagan pale stood mule-patient at the backs of gamblers with eyes only for queens of clubs and spades.

Drinks formally attired in condensation-dewed jackets festered on water-logged napkins. Cigarette and cigar smoke thickened into blue stairways to the shining chandeliers above.

On the baccarat dias, roped off by wine velvet cords, millionaires dropped five-thousand bets like dollar tips.

Darcy edged around the casino action and down the administration office corridor, slipping into Van's office and flipping on the light switch even before the wavering pool of flashlight in one corner had registered on her brain.

The room leaped into life in all its familiarity, including the icon of a black cat upon the desktop. The two strange men outlined against the window froze for a moment, then leaped toward Darcy and the light switch as if launched by pogo sticks.

Her hand had adhered to the plastic switch. Time slowed to a lazy melting moment. Then the warm passage of another hand paused on hers, gently pulling down, dousing the light.

She screamed her shock as careening men collided in the darkness.

"The lights!" a male voice commanded.

Darcy flipped them on again. Three men occupied the room now, the third stranger only slightly more familiar than the first two. He wore a wine velvet evening jacket and black satin bow tie. His right hand bulged the jacket's pocket and nudged in the strangers' direction.

"Better skip, mates," said the man from Van's office the other day, "or I'll have the house cops down on you."

They gauged his pocket-concealed hand first, then his eyes, and saw steel in one or the other, or both. Their hard faces hardened further before softening slightly. They shuffled out, not looking at Darcy, not making any noise.

"Why didn't you hold them?" she demanded a full minute after their departure, breaking the breathless silence.

Instead of answering, the man raised his fist from the pocket. Clutched in it was a fresh deck of cards stamped

the door. She paused halfway out into the bright afternoon sunshine to take one last look at her sleeping prince. Oh, fudge! Her journal and Steven's pages.

She ran back for the sheaf of papers, slapped it atop her acid-green notebook, and held them like a sloppy sandwich in indecisive hands. Van's informal office safe-deposit box was out of bounds to her now. She could hide them in her locker, but . . . if anyone saw Steven's writing when he'd entrusted it to her and even she didn't want to read it! . . .

She slapped them both into the briefcase, shut it, and slid it behind the loveseat. They could discuss it later. She suddenly realized what "later" would be—when Sirene returned from the last show. Maybe he would have repented and gone home by then.

Or maybe he'd still be here, waiting with a shaven face and hungry eyes to take Sirene (the painted hussy) into his arms. Darcy's internal early-warning system shivered in sheer excitement, even though she now heartily begrudged Sirene her role as sole recipient of Steven's affection.

Sighing, Darcy slipped out the door again. *Oh, what a tangled web and all that jazz,* she snarled to herself. Darcy McGill was dying to have Steven Austen right where she wanted him. And Sirene, that seductive figment of her imagination, her proxy doxy, was as close as Darcy would ever get to attaining that consummation so devoutly to be wished.

It was, she concluded, restraining herself from slamming her car door as she left the lot, driven out of her own apartment, a rotten world—especially if you had gone out of your way to insure that.

♥ Chapter Fourteen ♥

"Got an urgent message from an admirer, Darcy."

Jake's words barely checked Darcy's long-limbed flight toward the dressing room stairs. She teetered to a stop at their very top and glanced back over her shoulder.

"I'm late for a very important date," she objected, prancing impatiently from foot to foot. "With an opening curtain. Admirers can wait."

Jake, like most stage door guards, was a retired sedentary type whose gun holster barely buckled under a gravity-dropping belly symptomatic of beer by the six-pack and doughnuts by the carton. He waved a slip of beige hotel paper without moving to hand it to her. "It's from that Solitaire guy. I didn't know he was sweet on you."

"He's not. And it's mutual." Darcy grimaced indecisively. "I'll get it after the show. Now, I gotta fly!"

She did just that, letting her sure feet tap out her haste on the long flight of stairs. She shouldered past canvas-draped costumes on their hallway pegs and shot into the dressing room.

"Golly, Darce; we were about to call out the Mounties."

"Funny, Jo. I'll make curtain." Darcy slammed herself into her chair and began smearing on pancake. "Oh, Louie . . ." She looked helplessly at the cat ensconced on its cushion. "You're in my way!" She gave the pillow a rough shove into Jo's territory.

"Everything okay?" Midge's eyes reflected anxiety into her mirror image.

"Frankly . . ." Darcy paused, considering the day's happenings. "No. But I spent the afternoon buying up the west shopping mall, so I'm bound to feel better tomorrow."

"Oh, I got the neatest thing there yesterday!" Trish, already painted and dressed, minced over to twist a tube of lipstick open. A violet stick of color exploded like a bullet from the silver case. "Wild, isn't it?"

"You're not going to wear it on stage?" Darcy demanded, carefully brushing on thick lip color from a small tin. "It'll probably go green under the lights."

"Of course not; it's strictly for daytime—you know, something conservative."

Darcy rolled her eyes and settled down to gluing the black awnings of her false eyelashes into place.

"Better let Darcy play catch up," Midge advised in a commanding tone. "We can't afford to be one second off beat on our entrance, which is—" Her head cocked to the speaker.

"Three minutes, boys and girls," the stage manager announced on cue.

"—too soon," Midge said. "Come on, let's get Darcy's costume into fireman's jump-in order. We can find out why she's late later."

With the concerted aid of her stage sisters, within two minutes a fully made-up and fully semidressed Darcy was charging up the last flight of steps to the backstage area, grading herself for neatness of appearance in the door-mounted mirror and plunging into position with the other showgirls in the behind-the-scenes darkness.

In seconds, the orchestra revved up the overture, the curtain parted, and lines of dancers snaked into the blinding brilliance onstage. The show unwound like clockwork.

Back in the dressing room, Darcy pled schoolwork troubles and late assignments and hideous term papers for her dilatory ways. Then it was time to do it all over again. Sometimes being a showgirl felt like being a contestant on *Beat the Clock*, and like most TV game show contestants, showgirls often felt they came close to making fools of themselves. But none of the eleventh-second saves or close calls backstage showed.

Darcy shed costume after costume into the cheesecloth safety nets her dresser spread at her feet and donned the next begemmed installment without so much as a hitch of her pantyhose. When the show ran like a well-oiled machine, it didn't matter what emotional turmoil uncoiled in its components' hearts. At times like this, Darcy felt like an overdecorated automaton.

"I'm beat," she admitted in the dressing room after the last show.

While the others tore off their queen costumes and rammed on street clothes, Darcy dawdled at her mirror.

"I've got to check with Jake for a message anyway," she explained, yawning. It had been a long day of unexpected events, from premature rising to Fontana Family pow-wow to tucking in Stevenson Eliot Austen on her wicker loveseat.

Darcy absently pulled Midnight Louie's pillow back into proper position, apologizing for her earlier curtness with a head pat that the cat accepted without expression. "You're getting too fat and lazy to move," she complained fondly.

"Take it easy," Midge, the first out the door, said. Trish and Jo soon followed, leaving Darcy alone amid organized chaos at last.

She studied her mirrored self. Even that looked lead-faced. A three-sided frame of makeup lights was intended to banish shadows; instead, hollows clung stubbornly to Darcy's features, a look of loss haunting them. Shadows rubbed shoulders in the room reflected behind her, nestled behind hanging costumes and crammed into prop-jammed corners.

She didn't want to go home and couldn't decide if her reluctance came more from her fear that Steven might still be there, or her fear that he might not be there.

"Oh, Louie, could things get any worse?" she asked the dozing cat. He remained mum.

The sharp-edged bar of shadow visible through the crack in the dressing room door widened and then engendered its own shadow. Darcy straightened, watching the door in the mirror.

"Steven?" she whispered, tensing. Of course she should have realized he might have come here. Now there was no choice. Sirene was "on" again, like it or not, and Darcy was consigned to the broom closet of her own overinventive mind.

The shadow spit out its contents, a light-robed man with a dark bearded face. Darcy spun to see the stranger. Two others oozed into the room like clotted cream. Her true gentleman caller came last, blinking benignly through his thick-lensed glasses in the harsh lighting.

"You," Darcy breathed, standing.

Prince Idris-el-Shamsin, first son of the first wife of the Sheik of Abba Dhabba, stood there in his desert robes, his traditional headdress wound upon his head and circled with jewel-clamped twists of red silk. In a business suit, wearing his glasses, he would have been a nondescript man. Even in traditional dress he barely resembled the romanticized figure Darcy had etched in her Sirene stories. Yet power perfumed his presence, power taken for granted among rulers of an empty land suddenly oil-rich and populated with an illiterate, nomadic peasantry.

The prince snapped his fingers. A deferential servant advanced with a large shallow case, flourishing it open before Darcy with the air of someone unshielding a blinding uranium glare.

She gasped despite herself. A jeweled gold collar lay arranged on red satin, flanked by long gem-set earrings and underlined by a length of matching bracelet.

The gold alone made a fortune, dimpled with diamonds, sapphires, rubies, and emeralds at every conceivable joint, it totaled a sheik's ransom.

"I can't possibly—"

"You must," the prince said curtly. "It is my bride price for you."

"Bride price? But—"

"You will accompany me to Abba Dhabba. I will array you in splendor in my palace, among my wives and other concubines. You will be pleased to serve as my most admired treasure."

"I beg your pardon, Your Highness," Darcy said politely. Unlike the fictional Sirene, she had never stressed the difference in their height. "But I must decline. It is a most generous offer, and I am—" She glanced to the jewels; for all their worth, they were as overtly gaudy as the gold-foil-backed rhinestones she wore nightly. "I'm overwhelmed, but—"

"It is not an offer," the sheik's son articulated in his precise British accents. "It is an order. My men will take you quietly to my car and thence to my estate where a private jet awaits to escort us to Abba Dhabba. You will like it there— eventually," he promised as an afterthought.

"I'm a United States citizen."

"You are one of my retinue from this moment on. It is better to obey than to pay the price of not obeying." His chillingly matter-of-fact tones threatened only through implication.

Braced against the dressing table, Darcy let her long fingers hunt for a possible weapon. They stumbled over greasy open tins of clown-colored makeup, the long thin form of an eyebrow pencil, and a fat metal tube shaped like an oversized cartridge.

Trish's damn violet lipstick! Darcy realized, carelessly left, as usual, on someone else's table, just as Trish left everyone else's appropriated supplies on hers.

Long fingers expertly worked the top off, the lipstick up. Sideways, Darcy scrawled the shortest, simplest message her mind could manage. She didn't know if she had cancelled the painfully drawn letters by writing over them.

But when the prince's two men came to escort her out, she managed to roll the lipstick tube silently away in the general direction of Midnight Louie's concealing pillow. She cast the cat a farewell glance, then went to meet them, as meek as a lamb in five-feet-eleven hoofer's clothing, or lack of same, and followed the prince out into the empty hall.

Even Jake's post was momentarily deserted; once the shows were over, he didn't have to be there constantly. No one came or went in the back parking lot. It was two A.M. Night owls would be inside gambling fiercely; the early-to-bed crew had gone long before.

A limousine dark as the night itself purred at the door. The men rushed Darcy into the backseat, sandwiching her between the prince and one guard. Opaque windows emptied the night of even the routine reassurance of parking-lot lights. In utter blackness, the car whisked Darcy away into a bizarre future.

No one noticed. No one cried havoc. No one would

know until six o'clock tomorrow night that the Royal Suite Revue was missing one Queen of Hearts. Her long false fingernails creased her palms; if they had been daggers she would have used them. They weren't, and she didn't.

Steven lay in darkness, his neck and knees hanging over the edge of what seemed a table. He felt like someone the magician boxes in and saws in half.

When he moved his legs, his pooled blood tingled until he was convinced someone actually had sawed him off at the knees. But he finally sat up and felt the dark until his fingers found a lamp switch.

He blinked in the violent light. When had his living room sprouted chintz-covered furniture? Gradually, the paler blot of a door and a picture window registered on his senses. Darcy's apartment. He checked his luminous watch face. Four-ten. Had he slept since coming here at noon, then? His class! He lurched to his feet and blinked at the window again. The curtains were not drawn; the dark outside the glass was night.

Four . . . A.M. Good Lord. His glasses. Needed his glasses to think. His disoriented gaze found them folded as neatly as a grasshopper's hind legs on the coffee table.

"That's better," Steven told himself encouragingly. He felt hung over without the aid of alcoholic spirits. "Now that's a helluva waste," he chided himself, rising to turn on all available lights and study the situation.

No one occupied the bedroom he had shared once with Sirene. Perhaps she had gone out with friends following the last show. He backed away from the conflicting memories it contained, part rapture and part denial, and turned to the closed door Sirene had casually indicated was Darcy's room.

He opened the door slowly, then stopped, stunned. A yellow ten-speed bicycle gleamed in the light that leaked from the living room. Shelves held spare blankets and old magazines. It was a storage closet.

"Darcy's room," he told himself, where she supposedly had retired at his request to read his blasted scribblings. A storage closet? Darcy didn't live here? But he had found her here! Curiouser and curiouser.

Steven shook his head. Sleep had slowed him down, not restored his wits. But he had talked to Darcy—sixteen hours before. He'd given her his manuscript. Now, where was that? If he couldn't find that he'd really think he'd lost his blasted academic mind.

He finally found the briefcase behind the loveseat and, sitting, yanked it open on his knees. Besides the prolific proof of his writing binge, another sheaf of papers came out, bound in Day-Glo green. Its outré color intrigued him enough to flip open the notebook. It split with familiar ease to a particular page.

Steven recognized the handwritten sincerity of a writer's journal. He shut the page quickly, thought, then opened it again. Something was wrong, and if he had to do wrong to find out what, he would. Reading Darcy's journal was a slimy thing to do, but then Sirene had admitted to sneaking a peek, and something might be at stake.

He read the last entries, dated two days before. His eyes enlarged even more behind the magnifying lenses. The words sizzled into the crenelated hide of his brain, not because they sang, but because of what they said:

"I don't know what to do to get out of this mess, but one thing's clear: Sirene has got to go. She has become a monster that stands between me and everything I care about—all right, be honest, Pen—between me and Steven. I can't stand the idea of her making love to him anymore, which is pretty weird, but it's how I feel.

"Maybe Sirene could go on a boating jaunt with Prince Idris-el-Shamsin on Echo Bay and drown tragically when a kid on a Jet-Ski rams the boat. Or I could get her out to Hoover Dam and have her fall fatally from a sightseeing parapet.

"I like the Lake Mead idea best; it's deep and quite logical that a body would never be found there. . . ."

There was more, but Steve couldn't read it. His vision blurred as adrenaline poured into his sleep-numbed fingers, feet, and brain.

"Good God! Holy Hemingway!" He pushed the glasses atop his head and rubbed his eyes. "She's going to kill her sister! Over me. Oh, my God!"

He was up, patting for car keys in his pants pockets, leaving all the apartment lights blazing and the door agape behind him as he raced into the car-crowded parking lot, trying to find his own.

Maybe Darcy had decided to eliminate Sirene tonight, Steven worried. Maybe that's why she was gone and Sirene hadn't returned home yet. She mustn't do it! She must be stopped, or it would all mean nothing. All or nothing.

He couldn't think what anything meant, only that he had to save Sirene. The Accord started with a confident grumble. He screeched it out of its slot and guided it into the still-busy early-morning Las Vegas streets with mad, fully conscious recklessness.

Jake was waiting on watch behind his desk like a domesticated Cerberus at the gates of Hades.

"Oh, it's you, Professor. You're a little late tonight—or

The limo had impaled itself in cactus and creosote bushes to the hubcaps. Men scurried like ants around a collapsing hill, and the vast empty desert extended in all directions to the mountains.

"There's the highway." Steven pointed to a dull gray line bisecting the drab Mojave landscape.

"Well, you've rescued me. What do we do next?"

"Find someone to rescue us."

"Dare we rest first?" she asked hopefully.

He turned, doffed his glasses to wipe them on his shirt, then redonned them and studied their balked pursuers.

"In the next dry wash, I think."

She gave no argument, not even when he heeled the mare and it lurched down the incline at an impossible angle, nearly jolting her over Steven's back to the rocky cactus-studded earth.

She sighed and shut her eyes. It seemed over now—the fear, the insanity of her abduction, the wild, madcap escape. It seemed over in a very nice way, even if her muscles would rack her for it in the morning.

Sudden stillness interrupted her daydreaming. The living rocking horse beneath her had stopped moving.

"Can you slide off?" Steven was asking solicitously.

"Sure." She tumbled boldly to the ground, then felt her bowed legs wobble. Steven's strong arm was there to balance her; after all, she weighed much less than an Arab mare.

He walked the mare into the shade of an overhanging rock and ran a hand along her sweat-darkened side. "Not too bad. I'm sure Nostradamus went for help when he saw the smoke. They'll find us before it's too late for any of us. Watch out for snakes!"

His sudden warning couldn't keep her from wobbling

over on her sadly scuffed dancing shoes, and throwing her arms around his neck.

"Steven, you're a hero! I never dreamed that anyone could help me—that you could! Steven, I love you!"

She proved it by sinking a rabid kiss onto his surprised mouth. "Oh, Steven, when we get home, I'm going to abduct you into my *boudoir* and hug you and kiss you and call you my very own forever and ever. His Royal Pain didn't know the first thing about collecting uniquenesses, compared to me."

His mouth hardened under hers. Hands pried her arms from around his neck. He pushed her away, breathing harder than the effort required.

"Sirene, I'm . . . I'm sorry. I know you're grateful and a little crazy at the moment, but—"

" 'Grateful'! You call this grateful?" She plastered herself to him again, smiling to feel his repelling hands suddenly clasp her arms.

"Grateful," he said firmly, wrenching his face away. "Sirene, listen. You're a very attractive woman and all—"

"And *all?*"

"But I can't be your lover anymore."

She leaned away, blinking her shock with artificially supplemented lashes. They had clung faithfully through every trial.

"The prince didn't, didn't . . . do . . . something?" she asked.

"No!" He looked as shocked as she. "No, not that. You've got to understand, but how can I make you? Sirene"—he took a deeper breath then when he had faced the impending bulk of Ibrahim—"Sirene, I can't love you. I love Darcy."

"Darcy? *Darcy?*"

"Now don't be upset. I know she's your sister; perhaps that just makes it worse. But you see, I loved Darcy all along. I just didn't know it. Otherwise, I'd have never . . . never—"

"Friday night?" she inquired icily despite the sun-heated sand and stone oven in which they stood.

His face folded like a poker player's last hand.

"I'd never have made love to you if I'd admitted to myself that it was really Darcy I cared for," he tried to explain. "But you were so seductive, and you seemed to delight in pushing me to it. I was weak before, but I won't be weak now. Don't you see? We've both hurt Darcy very much. I even think she's, she's unhappy enough to contemplate harming you!"

"Darcy?" Sirene sounded even more dumbfounded than before.

Steven winced at the ugly revelations before him.

"I happened to skim some of her journal. She wrote of planning to 'get rid of' you, of a fatal boating accident on Lake Mead. She may need professional help. I'm afraid she's going to need all our love and support."

Sirene pushed off of him, tilting her face accusingly. "You read Darcy's diary?"

"Well, you did too!" he accused back.

"I guess I did." Sirene smiled and moved away, gauging his relief with every step back she took. She thought, visibly, looking from the ground to the sky to the mare. Then she looked at him again, challengingly.

"Steven, if I was such a problem to you and Darcy, why didn't you let Prince Idris's jet whisk me off into the Arabian Nights future he planned? I would have been out of the way forever."

"It . . . never occurred to me. At first, I was afraid Darcy was going to hurt you. When I found that someone else endangered you, I couldn't think of anything but getting you back. You've done nothing but follow your instincts all along. I'm the one that's been untrue to everything I believe in," he added distractedly. "You've a right to hate me, Sirene, and so does Darcy."

"But I don't, Steven," she said soothingly, advancing on him with all her glitter jingling. "I love you."

"You can't," he said hoarsely, trying to claw her arms from around his neck. "It's merely a carnal attraction, a passing whim."

She nibbled lightly at his neck, her fingers walking up his chest.

"Darcy's so ordinary," she pouted. "Darcy's dull, face it, Steven. Too dull for a bold, adventuresome man of the world like yourself. Would Darcy kiss you like this? See, you don't need Darcy at all—"

"But I do!" He wrestled free. "She's sweet and intelligent. We like the same things, books and writing."

"Have you ever slept with her?"

"Of course not! I've been, er . . . true to you, so to speak."

"A bird in the hand," Sirene purred, insinuating herself into his arms again, "is worth a question mark in the bush."

"No!" He pushed her off again. "Even if Darcy and I should . . . get together—and it isn't what you and I have had—I'll just have to live with that, Sirene. Sex isn't everything, but love is. You've got to stop this game. That's all it is to you, and I'm easy prey. But I'd never have succumbed to you if I hadn't been yearning for Darcy all along and not daring to admit it. My own student, for heaven's sake!"

"Well, you're in trouble now, buster." Sirene pulled away, it seemed for good. Her eyes flashed bolts of anger.

"Sirene, you won't tell Darcy about us?"

"I don't have to, Steven." Her head shook with disgust, making the golden earrings chime. "She already knows." A wicked smile parted her still-glossed lips.

"Steven, my love," She pinned him against the rock again, her smiling eyes and lips drawing so close they paralyzed him.

"I *am* Darcy!"

♥ Chapter Sixteen ♥

"Idris'll be long gone by the time the police get there," Darcy said.

"Yes," Steven said.

"I'm glad they didn't ask too many questions." Her fingers toyed with the golden necklace flashing across her collar bones. "They didn't even notice this."

"Yes," Steven agreed quietly. "I hope Nostradamus won't have any trouble getting the mare back to my place."

"What that little guy doesn't know about horses would rattle around like wax in a flea's ear. Will . . . Quaker like company?"

"He's a stallion and she's a mare."

"Well." Darcy sighed mightily and gazed out her apartment window, which was dark again except for a welt of sunset in the far west. "I guess it's finder's keepers. You get the horse and I get this clunky set of jewelry."

"Call it 'victim compensation,' " Steven said wryly.

They separately unreeled the day's events in their minds. Despite Nostradamus's rapid return with Macho Mario's limo and every vehicle owned by the Fontana boys, which amounted to a well-polished fleet, it had taken hours for the two parties—one mounted, one wheeled—to find each other, exchange stories and decide on a mutual plan of action.

In the end, Darcy and Steven had ridden back to Las Vegas in the limo. Nostradamus had taken horse and Honda in hand, promising to convey both to Steven's desert home unscratched. The Fontanas had revved their way forward to the Prince's ranch, vowing retribution.

It was left to Macho Mario Fontana to call the police and report the kidnapping, a role he cherished contemplating as he rode back into Las Vegas with Steven and Darcy, plying them with Napoleon brandy from his built-in-bar despite their demurs.

By the time the police had taken their statements and returned them to Darcy's apartment, it was nearly dark again. Their respective employers had been notified of the reasons for their absence—roughly, in Steven's case—both swearing to return to their jobs tomorrow. They were both wearier than Rodney Dangerfield's punch lines and Steven was beginning to look like one of the bearded Smith brothers, either Trade or Mark.

"So you never did read my . . . manuscript?" Steven asked, leaning forward on the wicker loveseat to pull the bricfcase to his knees.

"Steven. Will you ever forgive me?"

"For not reading my manuscript?" he joked uneasily. "Perhaps someday."

Darcy knelt beside him, her hands stopping him from delving further into the dark case.

"Not that! For . . . deceiving you, for pretending to be something I wasn't."

"But you were exactly what you purported to be! If I hadn't been so blind"—he angrily pushed his glasses against his forehead—"I would never have fallen for that Sirene act. Besides, maybe it wasn't an act. I don't know who the real you is, Darcy. I don't even know if I'd like her if I finally recognized her."

She sat back on her heels. "I thought you told me you loved me, out on the desert."

"I told Sirene I loved Darcy!" His hand distractedly

brushed his forelock over his forehead. "But now I find I've been making love to Darcy and talking nonsense to Sirene. I'm hopelessly confused. Hopelessly."

"Maybe if you read my journal—" She pulled the vivid green notebook into the lamplight.

"No!" His hands jerked back as if from an adder. "I don't want any more insight into what goes on in your schizophrenic head; I'm muddled enough already."

"We could have an exchange of hostages," she cajoled, pulling the fat set of typed pages from the briefcase. "Manuscripts at thirty paces. I'll go into the bedroom and read yours, if you'll read mine."

Steven snatched for the papers, but reckoned without Darcy's long arm and quick reflexes.

"Sirene—!" he began, then stopped. "You see; that's a trick Sirene would pull, whisking away something from under my nose. How am I to know when you're being you or when she's cropping up again?"

"Maybe we're both me," she said impishly. A laugh began effervescing in her throat. "Don't you see, you can have the best of both worlds?"

"When I see you in that get-up," he groused, lowering his glasses to frown at the faded costume, "it's hard to see anyone but Sirene."

She stood, a process that uncoiled as endlessly as when Darcy had described it in her first class assignment. Steven watched her progression from inferior to superior position with begrudging interest.

"I'll change into something more comfortable, then," she offered. "Why don't you sit tight and do some casual reading? I'll retire to the bedroom to read your stuff and get rid of this caked pancake."

"I want to get home and clean up myself," he agreed,

opening the notebook gingerly. "Mind you, I don't approve of us peeking into each other's innermost thoughts."

Darcy fanned herself with his manuscript, her eyes narrowing dangerously. "Scared of what I'll find in here, Professor?"

"Scared of what I'll find in here," he returned. "Perhaps there's a third Darcy, an undercover agent for the CIA."

"I swear not." She raised her hand Boy-Scout style, a gesture he regarded dubiously from over his glass frames before lowering his eyes to the handwritten pages again.

Darcy paused on the threshold to her bedroom. "Uh . . . some of that stuff may be embarrassing. I wouldn't let just anybody read it. I wouldn't let you read it if I didn't think it was important."

He shrugged his shoulders into the cushion back and settled firmly into his task, looking much as he did in a classroom despite his *African Queen* five o'clock shadow.

Darcy smiled as she cast herself stomach first across the bed and began reading Steven's manuscript. He hardly was one to complain about multifaceted personalities, the way he had ridden to her rescue.

She yawned. The typing was almost perfect, even though it was obviously first draft work. Didn't Steven do anything imprecisely? She heard him clear his throat in the living room and guessed that he'd already come across one of her soupy physical descriptions of him. Her eyes shut wearily; despite her fatigue she could feel a blush mounting all the way to her false eyelashes.

Darcy shook the typed pages in a businesslike way and began reading, intent on keeping her mind on what his mind had produced. Somehow writing this had made Steven realize he loved Darcy; she had to understand why.

Twenty minutes later she turned the last page over,

blinked and looked up at the opposite wall. She pushed herself up and marched into the hall and right up to Steven, who was still attempting to decipher her handwriting and only halfway through his assignment.

"Well, you're right. You do love Darcy. It comes through like gangbusters in the character of the district attorney's daughter, whom your hero is wacky about. But Steven, only Sirene would wear fishnet hose with her Malloy Dress-for-Success suits."

Stephen stared up at her, dumbfounded.

"You didn't ask for a literary critique, but I'm giving you one anyway. There's more energy in this writing than anything academic I've seen since first grade. I think you should finish it, and then I think you should try to get it published.

"Last but not least, you've got a lot of nerve hanging me for having more than one side to my personality when you are rife with unsuspected depths, widths, and heights. I fell in love with Professor Stevenson Eliot Austen, but there are a lot more of you in there that I know nothing about and I'm not so sure I want to if one of them is the narrow-minded prig who thought showgirls weren't respectable. So put that in your Ivy-League pipe and smoke it!

"I'm going to wash this chorus girl out of my hair and then I'm going to go to sleep and forget I was ever dumb enough to get a crush on a man I knew nothing about, much less sleep with one who'll lose respect for me for wanting to do it!"

She slapped the manuscript to the cocktail table and marched out again. Steven watched her depart, stunned. He picked up the pages.

"You . . . you really think it's good? You like it?" he called after her.

early today; you missed her."

"Miss McGill is gone?"

Jake pushed the guard's cap back on his head to polish his spreading bald spot. "Yep. All's clear below. I just checked. Say, have you been on a three-day winning streak, or what?" Jake nodded knowingly at Steven's face.

Steven rubbed anxiety-numbed fingers over what was now a two-day growth of beard, then tore his hand away.

"Do you know of any reason why Miss McGill wouldn't go straight home?"

"I keep track of their comings and goings here, but I'm no after-hours guardian angel. Unless . . . Solitaire Smith in the baccarat room left a note for her. She said she'd see him after the show."

"The baccarat tables?" Steven demanded. Jake's nod was enough to propel him through the plain unmarked door that led to the back of the casino.

Even gamblers slacked off in the morning's wee hours. Some twenty-one and craps tables were closed. The baccarat area, announced by gold cursive letters a foot high, looked empty except for idle, black-tied employees.

"One of you gentlemen named Solitaire?" Steven asked as he approached.

They eyed his appearance. Steven glimpsed himself in a gilt-framed mirror. He looked etched in shades of gray, like Ray Milland in the old black-and-white film, *The Lost Weekend*.

"It's important."

"Who's asking?" The man who spoke was the only one attired in a burgundy velvet evening jacket. Steven turned to him as to a prophet.

"You left a message for Miss McGill tonight. Did you see her after the show?"

The man shook his dark head, offering no more.

Steven's voice lowered. "I'm an instructor of her sister's, at the university English department."

Solitaire looked quizzical. "I didn't know she *had* a sister."

"It doesn't matter! The point is I'm afraid Miss McGill might have . . . Darcy could have . . . something might have happened to her, man! What was your message?"

Smith leaned against a fluted white-stone pillar, as unmoved by Steven's desperation as the column itself. But his eyes probed, and finally he answered.

"We had a mob of high rollers at the tables a few hours back. A bevy of Arabs betting heavily. They, uh, they were speaking of a dancer one of them fancied. I thought I heard the name McGill. I speak a smattering of Arabic. That's all. I was going to tip her off."

"Oh, my God!" Steven enunciated clearly for the third time that night . . . morning, whatever it was. "The son of the sheik."

"You talking about an old film, mate?" Solitaire inquired.

"Yes, an old film," Steven returned. Who would believe his wild story? No one who hadn't read Darcy's tales of Sirene and the sheik's son, Steven told himself. "I think I'll"—he looked around distractedly—"I think I'll have to find her myself. Thanks."

"No trouble," Solitaire Smith offered. "But if I were you, I'd get some sleep. You look like you've gotten a facial from a kangaroo."

"Sleep, sure. I'll do that." Backing away, Steven caught his balance at the top of a small flight of stairs and retreated under the dubious stares of the baccarat referees.

In moments he was back before Jake.

"I thought I'd . . . check downstairs. Just in case. That all right?"

"Sure, Professor, as long as you don't dress up as the Queen of Clubs, I don't care what you do down there."

"Right." Bowing away in a manner meant to imply extreme insouciance, Steven raced down the stairs the moment he was out of the guard's sight.

Luckily the overhead fluorescents had been left on for the cleaning crew. Steven could hear trash cans banging from the far corners of the understage rat's maze. He found the dressing room easily.

The room was empty, as Jake had said. Steven stared disconsolately at hanging maribu boas and sagging rhinestone bras. Among the preponderance of rainbow-colored feathers, he finally spotted one object that was not plumed or sequined or rhinestoned.

"If only cats could talk," Steven said, recognizing the big black mascot that had perched in exactly that position during his first encounter with the overwhelming Sirene. "Eh, kitty?"

The animal's self-satisfied face seemed to flinch at this form of address, but Steven was a horse-and-dog man himself and had never had much luck reading feline reactions.

The creature stretched out a languorous paw, then batted at a small gold case, its ears flattened and white whiskers pressed back against its jet-furred muzzle.

"That's a good, playful kitty," Steven told it, sighing as he studied Sirene's abandoned chair and litter-strewn tabletop.

The cat gave the object a sudden savage blow. It rolled toward the table rim, and Steven, being orderly, instinctively stooped to catch it in his palm.

But it stopped before rolling off the edge, and when he

picked it up, the shining surface was sticky. Steven looked down to the tabletop. There, scribbled in violet greasepaint, were two cryptic words. "Help, shieks!"

Steven stared. Clearly, Sirene couldn't spell well, but sheiks . . . The son of the sheik had returned! The Idris-el-Chamois from Darcy's journal. Darcy had nothing to do with Sirene's disappearing act—yet. It was only, only a wealthy, single-minded, spoiled son of the sheik of Abba Dhabba!

"Oh, my God!" Steven pocketed the lipstick, patted the cat thanks and darted out the door and up the stairs.

He had to do something, tell someone, go somewhere, but no course rang clear in his mind. Poor Sirene, in the hands of the scion of a patriarchal society where females were traded like baseball cards! Poor sheik's son . . . in the clutches of a mesmerizing manipulative specimen of the eternal feminine.

Jake was chatting at his desk with a slight, nondescript man. Steven clattered past them, their words catching up to him with dreamlike clarity.

"I'm not placing any bets this week, Nostradamus," Jake was saying firmly. "I'm still flat from last week. Those nags couldn't—"

Jake looked up. A harried Steven had materialized before him again. "I thought you left, Professor."

"Did you say 'Nostradamus'? *The* Nostradamus."

"Sure, but—"

Steven commandeered the little man's arm and dragged him to the door. "Nostradamus, come here; I need you."

"Hey, buddy, watch out for these delicate threads." Outside, the man shook off Steven's grip. "You wouldn't be collaring me for the feds?"

"No, Nostradamus, I'm worried about Miss McGill. My

name is Steven Austen; I'm a friend of hers. I just found a message in her dressing room about sheiks. Do you know about the rich son of an Arab sheik, who likes to gamble? Idread-el-Camel or something. I think he may have kidnapped her."

The little man blinked and wiped his forehead with a red bandanna he produced from his pantspocket.

"I know every dude who lays cards down on felt. If he messes with a showgirl, it's a rum hand he's dealt."

"Exactly. So who is this guy? And where does he live?"

Nostradamus sank his pointed chin in his palm and ruminated for a moment. Then his glance flashed up bright and on target.

"This dude has a spread where he raises the nags. I know where it is. We'll tail the scalawags!"

"Wonderful!" Steven pounded the bookie on the back, beginning to realize that there was something vaguely familiar in the way the small man phrased his replies.

"How far is it?"

"If you've got handy wheels, we can be there by morning. We'll drop from the dark and grab 'em sans warning."

"I'm, ah, delighted that you agree we should handle this ourselves. It really wouldn't do to include the authorities before we had proof. Then you're game to guide me there?"

"With what I know now, you couldn't stop me, mister. Why, I love that little showgirl like she was my sister."

"Yes. Er, I'm . . . quite . . . close to her as well. *And* her sister."

"Sister, mister?"

Nostradamus cocked his head, perplexed, but Steven swept him to the Accord.

"Stout fellow," he muttered while starting the engine. "If

Custer had had a dozen like you, I'm sure Little Big Horn would have been a different story. Ah"—Steven hesitated before entering the traffic flowing along the Strip—"one thing. Do you think you could knock off the rhyming—diverting as it is—when you're giving directions? You might lead me astray."

"No way," Nostradamus answered flatly. "Jose." He smiled.

Nodding numbly, Steven eased the car into the mainstream, then quickly sped onto the highway out of town, north to the empty desert. He was unhappily certain of where Sirene was, he reflected, but what the devil had become of Darcy?

♥ Chapter Fifteen ♥

". . . where the dawn comes up like thunder, on China 'cross the bay."

Steven crouched behind a rock-strewn rise, watching the sunrise gradually color the cold gray desert terrain to the shade of a dimpled brown pancake.

Beside him, Nostradamus glanced over quizzically.

"The line's from an old song, *The Road to Mandalay*," Steven clarified absently. "I'm afraid we're on the road to come-what-may." Steven nodded, his lenses winking in the concentrated light, to the nearby ranch house nestled into its sheltering oasis of trees.

Ghost-pale gray horses stirred in the grassless, fenced desert turf now that the sun was up, milling expectantly around their troughs. Unless humans kept livestock fed, watered, and shaded, they found the Mojave Desert a stingy mother to all but the few wild and wily mustangs and burros.

These horses looked well-tended and sleek. Their dawn-limned silhouettes showed them to be dish-nosed and dainty-hocked.

"Arabians," Steven muttered again. "Logical. But what's that structure behind the ranch house? It looks like El Rancho Minaret."

Rapidly warming sunlight gilded the edifice's bulb-topped towers and cast strong shadows into its pierced-pattern tiles. It also revealed the building's shape below the architectural decorations—a smooth windowless bunker of pale stucco, ominously featureless except for a wide-

185

timbered door. Before it, two robed men paced back and forth beside a long obsidian-sleek limousine, rifles cradled in their arms and caftans whipping like sailcloth in the morning breeze.

"It's a stronghold," Steven concluded aloud, "that's what it is. And that's *where* she is. I'll go down, you stay here, Nostradamus. If I don't return in a reasonable time, go for help. Take my car."

Nostradamus' mouth opened.

"No reasons, no rhymes," Steven forestalled him. "We haven't time to calculate scansion or debate the masculine or feminine rhyme schemes. This is my mess; I'll have to muddle through it. But thanks for showing me the way to"—he glanced again to the bleak bunkerlike structure—"to Medina on the Mojave."

With a brisk nod and a last push of his glasses to the bridge of his nose, Steven boosted himself over the rise and began the long walk across creosote bush-dotted desert to the prince's headquarters.

Nostradamus sighed, casting his eyes up at the rapidly blueing sky. No gods of gambling held celestial sway on this pitiless desert, where pockmarks and sinuous swirls in the sand revealed the nocturnal passage of its native creatures—vipers and rats.

"I'd say his odds are twenty to one," Nostradamus told the grave, unblinking lizard who had popped its head out of a rocky burrow to soak up some sun. "The university can write off a favorite son."

In the vast panorama beyond the rise, Steven was diminishing into a small moving figure. The horses neighed welcome as he passed their feeding station, lifting twitching noses to display buck teeth. Shortly after, the guards gave a ritual greeting, too, with lifted rifles focused on his breast-bone.

Nostradamus waited to see no more. He skittered down the rise, further scuffing the sides of his cream patent leather wingtips, scrambled into the car, and sent it lurching back along the empty, rutted road to town and some kind of help.

Steven, hands raised shoulder-high, approached the guards.

"How do you do? Lovely morning for a walk, isn't it? Ah, kindly tell His Highness that Professor Austen is here to see Miss McGill."

The glowering sun-scorched faces screwed themselves further into brutal disinterest. A rifle barrel rudely prodded Steven in the chest.

"It's impolite to point," he objected mildly. "Please inform your . . . er, master that I wish to speak with him."

They surveyed his unshaven face, his sand-scoured slacks and rock-scraped palms. Then one shrugged, shouldered his rifle by its leather sling, and vanished behind the wooden door.

Steven smiled winningly at the remaining rifleman and reached into his pocket. The rifle muzzle followed, pressing a perfect circle of threat against his flesh.

"Matches," Steven explained, cautiously pulling out a gold-embossed slick navy matchbook from the Crystal Phoenix. "I forgot they were in this shirtpocket, isn't that odd? Of course, I have no pipe to light—" He looked up as the other Arab returned and gestured him into the shadow of the open door. "Well . . . cheerio."

Steven waved the outside guard good-bye while tucking the matches behind his thumb and followed the other man into the welcoming dim interior.

Sand, tracked in on his shoes, grated with his every step on the cool white tiles underfoot. The walls were composed of intricate pattern-pierced blocks that allowed only the most abstract shards of light and sound to penetrate the corridor.

Steven was led through a veiled arch into another circular corridor. He moved about forty feet down the second passage before being ushered through an archway into yet another ring of hallway. This one stretched room-wide and was furnished with Oriental throw rugs, floor-set pillows, and a high-tech array of the latest audio-video equipment.

Onward and inward they went. Steven's methodical mind soon graphed the arrangement of this architectural madness. The place coiled like a maze, a round maze. To get in, one bore left at each archway; to get out, the opposite trend should work. He cataloged that fact on the assumption that this latterday set of Hansel and Gretel would have to make do without bread crumbs.

Now for the gingerbread house and the oven, he thought wryly, ducking another gauzy hanging and entering the huge circular central chamber he had anticipated.

"Steven!" Sirene's voice wailed in a dirge of startled dread.

She sat on a pillowed highrise across the room, glittering in her Queen-of-Hearts ensemble. A brighter, richer gleam shone from the bejeweled gold pieces glinting at her neck and wrist, and dangling from her ears.

Around her, the room unrolled like an Arabian Nights tapestry—richly hung with fabric and color and the winking glint of brass and gemstones. On a dais at the room's far end sat an upholstered baby-blue crushed-velvet cocoon—the largest, gaudiest, most self-indulgent king-size waterbed Steven had ever seen.

Its very presence struck horror into his heart.

A short man, bespectacled like himself, held court on an X-chair centered in the space. He immediately noted the direction of Steven's gaze.

"Splendid waterbed, is it not? It has color TV, stereo headboard, VCR, and a telephone, all built in. I ordered it at the Furniture Market in San Francisco, and they customized it especially for me. There is no other like it in the world."

"I'm sure of it," Steven said fervently.

"I collect," the prince further explained, "that which is one of a kind, I think you call it. You Americans are so ingenious with your technology. Everything here is big, bigger, biggest." He glanced at Sirene in her pillowed splendor. "Even your women."

"Yet this one"—Steven let his eyes stray to Sirene—"is a little, er, skinny. I thought the discriminating Arab preferred robust women."

The prince shrugged. "My eye has been educated to Western standards in some things. My Sirene remains a worthy collectible."

"Of course, of course," Steven soothed. "I never meant to question the wisdom of Your Highness's . . . investment."

The prince laughed and leaned forward, his beringed hands spread on his robed knees. "Of course you did, Professor. You came here to bargain her back, did you not?"

"Bargain implies an exchange. I am empty-handed." Steven showed his palms. "I came to persuade you to free her."

"Free? She *is* free. I have chosen her; what else would the woman want?"

Steven wet his lips. "That is not our custom."

"I . . . customize . . . your customs, Professor." The prince's smiling face grew taut. "My father is a collector as well—of American professors, whom he pays handsome sums to teach the royal sons of Abba Dhabba. Do not seek to outwit me. I know the turnings of such minds as yours."

"Outwit you? Never! I come only to entreat you, beneficent prince that you are, to return this woman to me."

"Ah." The prince lavished a wasted triumphant glance on his stone-faced retinue. "Now it becomes interesting." His voice snapped out the next words. "She was *your* woman, then?"

Steven glanced at Sirene, already suffering the indignity of captivity and now about to be argued over like a choice piece of sirloin.

"Yes . . . and no," he temporized.

"This is why you Americans lose influence the world over!" the prince raged. "This 'yes and no.' Was she or was she not?"

It occurred to Steven that the prince might mistakenly believe he had acquired a virgin. He swallowed—and committed truth.

"We have been lovers."

The prince roared with laughter. "And you think she would prefer to remain with you, rather than accompany me to my palace in Abba Dhabba?"

"Ask her."

Now the prince seemed at a loss. "There are some customs of Abba Dhabba it is best not to challenge," he finally said. "A woman's opinion is as a grain of sand: insignificant and yet likely to be a great irritant in the wrong place."

Sirene stirred indignantly, causing a great clatter of body

jewelry. Two guards implanted heavy hands on her restive shoulders.

"Steven, don't reason with this thug; just deck him," she suggested angrily.

Silence ruled the room. Steven sighed, knowing the uselessness of attacking the prince in his den. Prince Idris rubbed his short black beard with a hand on which every finger was knuckled with a ring, even to the thumb. A wicked gleam polished his olive-dark eyes.

"So. You say she is your woman. Perhaps. I say she is mine. Certainly. Would you fight for your woman, Professor?"

"I suppose so," Steven answered warily.

The prince beamed. "Would you fight . . . *Ibrahim!*"

The last word was a bellowed summons. From beyond a soft shimmer of translucent curtains came the bare-torsoed bulk of a gigantic man, his muscles hung with excess flesh, his harem trousers lacking only the usual accouterment of a curve-bladed sword at their sash. Apparently Ibrahim relied on personal force rather than metal weaponry.

"Well?" demanded the prince.

Steven swallowed. He'd never attacked anything more dangerous than a trespassing chuckwalla lizard. Now somehow his manhood was at stake as well as Sirene's future.

He advanced toward the hulking man despite her wailed "Steven, no!" from the sidelines. Then he paused as if to reconsider, turned, and walked back to Idris.

"Would Your Highness hold my glasses?" Steven asked, presenting them with a bow. "I wouldn't want Ibrahim to be accused of the cowardly act of hitting a bespectacled man."

This time the prince's laughter nearly shook the surrounding ring of curtains; the flames in the braziers before them seemed to shrink in the good-humored wind of it.

"I like you, Professor! I like you so much that I will take you, too, back to Abba Dhabba. Put on your spectacles and put aside heroics. The royal spawn are forever increasing and presently number one hundred and thirty-eight. My father can always use another American professor. What do you think of that?"

"I think that's better than nothing," Steven reflected quickly, polishing his glasses on his shirttail before redonning them.

Perhaps, in time, he could think of some way to free Sirene. In the meantime, of course, she would be at the beck and call of Idris-el-Chamois, a thought that filled Steven with rage enough to dispense with three Ibrahims.

"And as a boon," the prince was saying, "I will grant you the occasional opportunity to sample the lovely Sirene's delights. Is this not a fair settlement of disputed territory, my friend?"

A sound halfway between a gasp and a sob wrenched the silence. Steven didn't look around to find its source, but his hands tightened into fists.

"No, Your Highness. It is not fair. I would rather face a thousand Ibrahims than violate one woman in my power."

"But she was your lover. Surely, it would be the same."

"Not if she isn't free to refuse—either you, or me."

"What strange customs you have," the prince marveled. "Is the camel who bears me free? The servant who pours my wine? We must all compromise with life."

"Not in this."

Truly puzzled, the prince lowered his voice. "But consider, if she resents her fate, would not the hope of reuniting with a past lover lighten her mind? Although of course I foresee that she will soon come to love my royal self as much as my other concubines."

"Perhaps," Steven conceded. "But it would be a false surcease. I would never be a party to it."

"Hmmmm. Most interesting! We shall have to test that in Abba Dhabba."

"It's no use, Steven," Sirene cried from her side of the room. "He's used to absolute power; he can't know or care about honor."

"Silence!" His face clouded with anger, Idris rose. "I know honor; I merely do not grant your odd notions of it. We will go soon, and I will take only the woman. You incite her to rebellion, Professor, and as such are a dangerous man. Take him out!"

"Wait!" Steven's shout halted the guards coming toward him. "I'd like to say good-bye to her."

Idris' arms spread wide. "I am a civilized man. Of course. Then you go."

Sirene, subdued, was so white with fatigue that her makeup stood out against her blood-drained skin like an image applied over it.

Steven walked to her quickly. Her eyes followed him, luminous with unshed tears of pure fright. He put his hand to her shoulder, no more than the guards had done.

"Sirene, I—"

"I know you tried. I don't know how you found me, or how you came here. There's so much I have to tell you. Oh, Steven, there's no way out!" Her hands crept up to his.

"Hush. Just listen. Hard. There's a matchbook in my hand. Take it. When they're watching me leave, light the whole book and touch it to the curtains behind you. Then run like hell, and we'll try to get out."

She inhaled quickly, her tight fingers loosening to trace the shape of the matchbook under his hand.

193

"What do you say?" the prince demanded.

Steven turned, his fingers moving to the heavy necklace's jewel-brailled surface. "Just admiring Sirene's new jewelry."

"My gift," Idris agreed proudly. "Her bride price."

Sirene whimpered her rage and clasped the matchbook in her palms. Her eyes were lucent as they stared up into his, lucent and no longer apparently blue, Steven thought, as if all the color had washed out of her.

Patting her shoulder awkwardly, he stepped away. Immediately two custodial guardsmen slipped beside him. Their footsteps echoed on the tiled floor as they brought him before the prince one last time.

"Farewell, Professor," Idris bid with a wave of his gold-knuckled hand. "Do not consider going to the authorities over this. My reach is as long as my memory."

Steven's eyes dropped. He allowed the two men to grasp his arms as they turned him toward the exit. He paused suddenly, twisting his head over his shoulder.

"Your Highness! You said you were a collector of unique things. Did you know she had a sister—a twin sister? She is one of two. Sirene isn't unique."

"Two?" Idris rose, glowering. "None of my agents told me this."

"It's true," Steven said. "I teach her sister at the university. It's how I met Sirene. She's not one of a kind."

While Idris frowned indecisively and his retainers looked to him for orders, Steven's guards let their hands drop away. Across the room, a shout drew all eyes that way. A pyramid of flame was climbing the fragile curtains that ringed the chamber. Running from its fiery heart with agile doelike leaps, kicking flaming braziers over as she went, came Sirene, her face ablaze with freedom.

One guard tried to stand in her way, but a long leg performed the head-high chorus-line kick that ended the second act of the Royal Suite Revue. The guard received a royal knock on the chin that sent his weapon skating far across the slick floor to no one's good.

Steven snagged Sirene's hand in passing and dashed for the exit archway.

Smoke billowed the curtains behind them, but only sounds pursued them, confused cries and the bellow of an angry prince: "*Not* one of a kind?"

"This way!" Steven yanked Sirene to the right through another arch, running down the passage, then jerking her right again, running and veering right again.

They crashed through the wooden exterior doors, aware of feet drumming the floor behind them. The single exterior guard fell before the violently opened door. Steven, no longer thinking, pulled Sirene after him, heading for an oasis in the desert—the shade and shelter of the few trees grouped together—drawn to the creatures he knew.

The deceptively quiet stable was dim, but the subdued glitter of the tack room beckoned through an open door. Steven dove into the room and whipped a pair of bridles off their hooks. The cries of angry men escalated behind them. He took Sirene's hand again and led her out to the corral. In the shade of a salt cedar, Steven coaxed a startled white mare to statue stillness, then patted the wary muzzle. The bridle slipped on before the horse could lash her dainty head back to evade it.

"Steven, they're coming this way!"

He was up on the mare already, fighting for control as she spun in the rising sandstorm her hooves created. He dropped the second bridle to the sand and thrust one helping hand down to Sirene.

She stared at him, her Queen-of-Hearts red satin powdered white with dust, the swagging rhinestones winking in-congruously.

"You're kidding!"

"Come on!"

"Bareback?"

"Jump up!"

"Who do you think you are? Indiana Jones?"

Dust covered the windows of his glasses, obscuring his eyes. The nervous mare churned the soft turf, showing sickles of eyewhites. Footsteps pounded onto the wooden stable floor behind them.

She took the hand, vaulted into a balletic leap and found the hard hide of an equine derriere slapping her own. Steven pulled her forward against his back. He didn't have to tell her to hang on. She wrapped long arms around his midriff, then clasped her own wrists and pressed her face into the darkness above his shoulder blades.

The mare, released from the chaos surrounding her, bounded forward at the urging of his heels. A jolting trot quickly rolled into a canter and then the beast flew over the fence rail as if transformed into Pegasus.

Sand sprayed around them in clouds. Through the mist they saw smoke funneling out of the bunker and agitated men jumping into cars, foremost among them the long black limousine.

"They're crazier than you are," she shouted into Steven's back, but he didn't seem to hear. The great pounding beast under her was stretching sinuous running muscles; her thighs gripped the uncoiling power as if trying to ride a hurricane. Hooves skimmed the surface of the sand in rhythmic certitude. Lungs bred for endurance heaved mechanically.

At the top of a rise, Steven reined the mare for a moment to look back. Sand-mired jeeps spun in impotent circles.

The sound of the shower at full rush answered him briefly before a slamming door muffled the noise. Annoyed by her sudden exit, and even more by her truncated praise of his prose, he rose and followed her. Already steam sifted out from under the door. Steven envisioned a highly irate dragon stoking its fiery breath behind the hollow-core door.

He turned the knob and opened the door a nose-width.

"Ah . . . Darcy? Are you in there?"

"No! I just turned into Madame Tussaud."

"I, er, thought I'd borrow your electric razor—the one you showed me before. Before I went home."

"It's on the sink ledge."

He spotted it, hefted it, then regarded his semi-bearded face in the steam-clouded mirror.

"So you, you like what you saw?" he asked cautiously.

"I've always liked what I've seen, Steven," she answered briskly, her voice reflecting her movements under the hissing water.

"It's important to me," he answered. "What I wrote, what you think about it."

He let the razor, mute pretext for his presence, rest on the porcelain again beside the two soggy false eyelashes that lay in what seemed demurely closed position. The small wastebasket overflowed with used cotton balls tinted the exact red of Sirene's lips and cheeks. The blue of her eyes smudged several others. Steven had a horrible feeling, as if he attended a funeral of someone he had used to know very well—perhaps even himself.

"Darcy . . . is it really you in there?"

The shower curtain jerked back just enough for her water-dripping face to peer through.

"Of course it's me—all me, and only me."

"Your eyes . . . they've always been hazel," he marveled,

as if seeing them for the first time. "For a while, I could have sworn Sirene's were blue."

"You wanted to believe in Sirene as much as I did, Steven," she answered more softly. "I only invented her in the first place to fictionalize my life in your eyes. And I only brought her to life because — because you were standing in my dressing room wanting to be wanted so much it hurt me."

"Was I . . . that obvious?"

"No. But I understood you. I've felt the same way. I've always wished some bold prince charming would sweep by and sweep me into his arms. I never thought I'd have to be the one to sweep."

"But you liked it." His hand moved to shower curtain, just beneath where she clutched it.

"Careful! You'll get wet."

"I need to get wet."

"Not with your clothes on."

"Er . . . no. But they come off."

"And your glasses are getting all steamed up."

"Oh? I hadn't noticed."

"Honestly, you are so typically absent-minded. If I weren't around I don't know who would look after you. Well, take them off."

"My clothes?" he asked hopefully.

"Your glasses." Water sprayed unabated through the shower head. "Then your clothes." Her head whisked out of sight as she jerked the shower curtain shut.

It was an opaque white color with green waterlilies here and there. As Steven watched, he saw a shadow shifting like something underwater. A lilypad or two suffered a subtle bump.

His glasses were totally steamed up by now; he folded them on the sink ledge next to the abandoned eyelashes. He gave these last a regretful glance; they did have their uses and produced an elusive tickle.

He folded his pants over the empty towel rod, his shoes he set side by side beneath it. The shirt, mostly shredded, he draped over the sink along with his jockey shorts.

There was no more conversation from the bathtub. Nervously, he poked the shower curtain back. Darcy, her long brown hair water-plastered to her back and shoulders, was standing in the corner, away from the fierce drum of water, her hands behind her back. She looked so much like a child sent into a penitentiary corner that he smiled and stepped over the tub edge.

"There's really only one, sweet—somewhat shy—woman in here, isn't there? Where'd that hussy go?"

"Down the drain! Steven, we both know what we're doing now." Darcy's hands fanned against the wet white tile behind her. "There's nothing between us but us. We can't pretend the devil made us do it."

"Good. I'm ready to take responsibility for myself." He pulled her into his arms and directly under the messaging raindrops of hot, pouring water.

Their eyes closed as automatically as their faces turned up to the water's source and toward each other. Everything seemed to be moving—the water, the blood surging through their arteries, maybe even the earth far, far under their feet.

"This is a rather inconvenient time to say this," Steven went on after catching a deep breath. "But I've always loved you, Darcy; I love you now even more, and I always will." His fingers smoothed her sleek hair to her shoulderblades. "And I saw in your journal that you feel the same way and always have."

"Do I?" she asked blissfully.

He shook her. "Of course you do! Say you do."

"Oh, you're so masterful. Or should I say, doctorful? I do, I love you, Steven. Say something to me in Cavalier!"

"Ah—" Steven's gray eyes glazed as his academic mind dutifully sought a reference. "All I can think of is . . . 'liquifaction.' "

"Does that mean 'dangerous when wet'?"

"Very dangerous. Aha, I have the very verse—if you will remove your cherry-like lips from mine a moment so I can declaim it."

She obliged, resting her sopping head on his now-soapy shoulder.

> " 'Then be not coy, but use your time,
> And, while ye may, go marry;
> For, having lost but once your prime,
> You may forever tarry.' "

Darcy lifted her head cautiously. "Was that a proposal, Professor?"

He nodded. "I think so. I have a way with words, but those old-time versifiers got right to the nitty-gritty."

"I know, and I do and I will!" She threw her arms around his neck again, kissing him with an exuberance he quickly slowed to softer repeated offenses.

"Darling Darcy, you're going to have a hell of a whisker burn tomorrow."

"It is tomorrow. Let Sirene worry about it; she's the one who has to go on stage." He stood motionless in her arms. "Oh, I'm sorry! Is she persona non grata?"

His arms tightened. "She's always welcome to visit now and again, but I'd really rather have you around the house." Steven frowned. "And why weren't you listed on the revue program as Darcy McGill, anyway? If you had been, I might

210

have never fallen for . . . any of it." He kissed her wetly on the nose.

"Oh, that. Well, I told you the truth, as always, Steven. I was christened 'Ramona Catherine—R.C.' People started calling me 'Darcy' when I was a little girl. It stayed."

"And where did 'Sirene' come from?"

"My imagination, which you were always urging me to use in class."

"I think I'll use some of it now," he said definitely. "I'm going to name the Arab mare Sirene, and she's yours."

"Mine! My own personal white—well, gray—horse? With a knight in shining glasses to go with it? I can't tell you how happy I am!"

"Words, words, words," he complained. "Hasn't any writing instructor of yours, Miss McGill, ever explained that it's better to show, not tell?"

"It's lucky for you," Darcy retorted, "that I'm a fast learner."

She proceeded in the slowest possible manner to teach her professor a thing or two he was most eager to learn.

♥ Chapter Seventeen ♥

"Drat these eyelashes!" Darcy stripped them roughly from her lids and rolled them on a pencil. "They've never been the same since!"

Midge, Jo, and Trish, nearly ready to depart the dressing room for the night, or morning, rather, knew better than to inquire too closely into anything having to do with the events of almost a year before.

" 'Night, Darce," they chanted in turn and slipped out of the dressing room.

Midnight Louie, drowsing on his high-profile pillow, knew a lot more than they did, but was in no mind to mention it.

A moment later, the dressing room door burst open. Steven burst through.

"I couldn't wait for you to get home! Look what came today!" He tossed a paperback book with a rather gaudy cover featuring sultry women and granite-faced men toting heavy artillery on the cover.

Darcy regarded this with the amazed pride and joy usually reserved for one's firstborn.

"Oh, Steven, it looks wonderful," she cooed with fond satisfaction. "And they put Ned Bond *above* the title."

"Yes, well, I don't know about that title—"

"What's wrong with *Bullets to Bedsheets*? It's alliterative, catchy—it's got zing. Besides, the publishers must know what they're doing."

"I doubt that," Steven said, "but I'm having a lot of fun with this stuff. It's awfully liberating to do exactly what everybody told you not to do for years and years. If my university colleagues only knew I was the author of *The Nightprowler* series—"

Darcy jabbed one long red false fingernail into the mirror, where it stabbed a taped-up page from a magazine. "You academic peers certainly know what *I'm* up to." They spent a moment's silence beaming at the first of Darcy's Sirene stories to see print. The buyer had been *Playgirl* magazine, the price $1,500, and the byline was Darcy McGill Austen. "I just love it that your last name is spelled like Jane Austen's," she said dreamily. "I adore unlikely juxtapositions."

"Speaking of unlikely juxtapositions," Steven said, pulling her up from her chair, "I've got a chilled bottle of champagne in my briefcase outside the door. I suggest I bring it in, lock the door, and we celebrate."

"In here! How imaginative, darling." She wrapped herself around him. "But what about the cat?"

Steven glanced at the massively indifferent Louie. "He'll never tell."

In a minute he had the split of champagne open, Darcy had rinsed out two plastic drinking glasses at the dressing-room sink, and they were toasting their literary success.

"To Mr. Bond," Darcy invoked throatily.

"To Mrs. Austen."

They giggled together like impish children, then tilted their glasses jointly.

"What would they say at the faculty tea if they knew that the author of *Circle Symbolism in 'Moby Dick'* was also Ned Bond, author of *Bullets to Bedsheets*?" Darcy asked impudently.

Steven set their champagne glasses down and put his hands on Darcy's rhinestoned hips. "What would they say at the faculty tea if they knew that Mrs. Stevenson Austen, faculty wife and short fiction author, was a certified, rhinestone-G-string-wearing showgirl?"

"They'd probably say that appearances are everything, but I'd answer that it's what's underneath that counts."

"You are as incorrigible as your inestimable sister, the late great Sirene."

"Oh, Professor," she mocked tenderly, coming incorrigibly closer. "What big words you have."

♥ Chapter Eighteen ♥

Midnight Louie Performs an Epilogue

So there I am, trapped. I tell you, in all confidence, that I do not witness so steamy an occasion since I am near the sauna of the Apollo Health Club when Rats McCafferty takes a distinctly unhealthy dose of hot air, thanks to Georgie the Forgery jamming the exit door with a crowbar.

There is no describing what lengths people will go to in front of helpless witnesses from the animal kingdom.

Luckily, I am a dude about town and see more than a few cats on the Strip about their mating rituals, so I am beyond shocking. And I must say that now and again my thoughts roam to certain exploits of a sensual nature in my own past, including one energetic lady of the Siamese persuasion whose come-hither baby blues make me sing the blues in the night until I am dissuaded by some punks brandishing tire irons.

So I cannot blame the professor and his star pupil for carrying on in the dressing room, being it is so late at night that it is early in the morning and being that they are legitimately hitched in holy matrimony.

There is another lady of my acquaintance, Mehitabel by name—it may be you hear of her—who is a great believer in companionate marriage, which is everything but the ceremony. But she is ahead of her time, and I myself do think that there is nothing nicer than rings and vows and a little rice underfoot for the right people.

And Professor Steven Austen and the former Miss Darcy

McGill definitely seem like the right people for each other, although I will have to keep an eye on the career of this Ned Bond. It occurs to me that if Mr. Ned Bond becomes as popular a practitioner of the literary art as, say, Mr. Damon Runyon or Mr. Sidney Sheldon, there might be some money to be made doing what comes naturally . . . keeping my trap shut.

Not that I am thinking of shaking down a friend, but I am no spring kitten now and have to look out for my old age. I cannot sign Medicare checks with these busted paws—I have engaged in a few back-alley pugilistic exercises in my time, purely in the defense of a lady, of course.

Of course, if the professor is not willing to lay a few mackerels on my plate to keep my mouth shut, I might manage to pick up some sardines from the *National Inkquirer*, a journal of a gossipy nature that is always on the hunt for a juicy journalistic morsel or two.

It requires acting anonymously, but fame is not my game—I am a retiring fellow and, as always, impeccably discreet—and besides, a soupçon of bad publicity from a classy source like myself might do a lot of good for the professor's writing career.

♥ Tailpiece ♥

When Romance Meets Mystery, No Love Is Lost

At least in this book I am shown as enough of a house detective to present a clue to the proper party. I cannot imagine how it was possible for the first editor to cut my role by forty percent in this tome: my part must have already been down to the bare bones.

I had to take care not to let you "overdo" your role, Louie. I can see that I need to explain romance novel conventions to a dyed-in-the-pelt mystery dude like yourself. "Conventions" are nothing more than rules or formulas, and I wasn't used to writing by the rule book.

All genre fiction is "categorized," thanks to publishers and reviewers and even readers. In the mystery field, one of the major two modes is "crime" fiction: stranger-in-the-night scenarios; gritty, action-oriented stories about professional crime solvers—cops and PIs—pursuing hardened killers. The other mode is in the classic British tradition of Agatha Christie: killing-me-softly stories of murder among friends and family, which examine specific milieus, often satirically, and dwell not on the violence, but its cause and aftermath. Both warp "reality" in their own ways.

Books on the softer side of mystery are called "cozies," a term I find dismissive and sexist, as I said on a panel with Carolyn G. Hart, a dedicated scholar and writer of such books. She suggests using the term "traditional" mystery as less demeaning.

But, I answered, I've never done anything "traditional" in my writing life, either. All of my 38 books combine genres. It's no wonder I've run into editors who object to my literary recombinations.

So I've created a new term to describe your regular mystery series: cozy-noir. I'm sure you, being feline, like having things both ways as much as I do. You, by the way, Louie, are the "noir," and the four human characters in that series mix cozy and noir backgrounds and traits.

Of course I am noir through and through! *Noir* **is the French word for black, and I am your quintessential black cat, born to walk those mean streets unseen. But I also like to cozy up on a sofa to contemplate the hard lessons of life in a soft spot. Is that what you mean by cozy-noir?**

Not entirely, but it will do.

And what has this to do with that other French word, *l'amour?*

As for romance, the conventions in that field were the most stringent in publishing in the late seventies when the romance boom began. The choke-hold on content and style began to loosen in the eighties, but not for all romance publishers or all writers. I wrote the Quartet for perhaps the most "liberal" line then, and it's hard now to see from these books how cutting-edge they were. Here's some of the new "freedom" I had then: to write from male as well as female point of view; to use a narrator-cat, however lightly; to refer to sexual responsibility and contraception (AIDS was not yet public knowledge when I wrote these books).

It's interesting to see from the editor's cuts what I couldn't do, and *The Cat and the Queen of Hearts* is the book of the Quartet she had the most trouble with. Oddly enough—or not so oddly—it was the reader favorite. It's the writers' and readers' job to be ahead of the editors, just as when I was a newspaper reporter I knew what was happening on the street and on my beat (social issues, the arts and popular culture) and had to convince the office-bound editors that it was worth covering.

Here's what that editor objected to, which was outlined in the proposal she accepted: The professor hero wasn't "manly" enough, though my model was Cary Grant in classic film romantic comedies, and he was manly enough for several generations of women movie goers. Darcy's deception in playing her own sister was a problem too. Romance heroines never "lied," so I had to insert much interior agonizing over how Darcy was driven to do this against her better judgement and felt terribly guilty. When the professor finds out that Darcy is Sirene, he reacts with anger and confusion at being tricked. This normal human response was a no-no. The editor explained that he was delighted to have his cake and eat it too; that scene was cut.

This book, originally titled *Las Vegas Strip* because it involved two characters stripping down to their unspoken wants and needs despite how others might view them, was retitled the horribly trite *The Professor and the Showgirl*. This was so trite that another romance line published an exactly titled book the same season.

Yet the cliched title also demonstrates the classic, fabulist role of romance mythology, and why romances are so popular and necessary in our culture. To those inclined to sneer at romance novels, I point out that fiction that investigates how one half of the population learns to live with the other, especially when cultures world-wide make women second-class citizens to men, is hardly trivial.

Just as fairy tales help children address issues of powerlessness and growing up, romances do this for women, some with more sophistication than others, of course.

Romances are morality plays in which a woman and a man are forced to confront each other by the draw of sexual attraction to learn about each other and themselves, and about how to make a more profound alliance, despite social and personal obstacles. There are classic recurring themes that reflect the perils of very real life: the arranged (forced by circumstance) marriage, or, in this case, the Inexperienced (innocent) man maturing through a relationship with an apparently Fallen (sexual) woman. In the text, I mentioned the poem about *The Owl and the Pussycat* who went to sea, but a Broadway play by that name plays on the same tradition, as does a more obscure play, Charles Dyer's *Rattle of a Simple Man.*

I saw the marvelous Milo O'Shea in a performance at Dublin's immortal Abbey Theater during my epic college trip to Europe. I say "epic" because that six-week bus jaunt through countries from Ireland to Greece and Belgium to Portugal made me a novelist. In the first country we visited, Ireland, I witnessed an incident of English bigotry toward the Irish that spurred me to begin *Amberleigh* (my first novel, set in 1893 Ireland) when I returned to college that fall. I'm still exploring the Irish Troubles as a background factor for a major character in your mystery series, Louie, which will run a decade into the new Millennium. In the Quartet, Van von Rhine's hotel manager father springs from my serial stays in a slew of hotels far less posh than the ones she grew up in. When I used the web to find the playwright's name for *Rattle of a Simple Man* for this afterword, I found a short synopsis that begins: "Timid football fan Percy is down from Manchester with the lads and after the match is picked up by lovely young prostitute Cyrenne."

Amazing. My subconscious had dredged up that forgotten name when I created Darcy's supposed sister Sirene twenty years later. Sirene is a homophone, or sound-alike, for Cyrenne. I thought at the time that I came up with the name only as a play on the word "siren" and the title of a forties play and film, *My Sister Eileen.*

I researched showgirls during my first, 1985 trip to Las Vegas. Although the MGM Grand building I visited then is now Bally's, *Jubilee!,* the same extravagant show I portrayed in *The Cat and the King of Clubs,* still successfully plays there fourteen years later. The poem Darcy posts on the dressing room door in this book was copied from an actual posting then, so the anonymous and long-gone chorus girl gets credit. I was delighted to use the clever verse to underline the book's point that showgirls are dancers, not dumb-dumbs. It takes great mental as well as physical energy to dance.

And, by the way, Louie, lest your alleycat upbringing cry "foul!" at my youthful privilege in touring Europe, I hasten to point out that it was funded by a deferred benefit from my salmon-fisherman father's on-the-job death when I was a toddler.

Say, *my* father did time as house cat on a salmon-fishing boat in the Pacific Northwest too!

My, what a coincidence. Guess we were fated to collaborate.

Yeah. And far be it for me to sniff at the inclinations or abilities of others to gad about the globe. I might be interested in such broadening exercises myself, except that my beat is Las Vegas, where the management kindly brings the globe to me: the new Venetian and Paris being only the latest international sweetmeats on my all-American blue-plate special in the Mojave desert. The Venetian is more loaded with canals than Mars. So, what is with this fascination with water, anyway? Loathsome stuff, although fish swim in it, and for that I must be ever grateful.

W. C. Fields, the comedian, hated water for the exact same reason you tolerate it, and thus turned to drink. Water is an attraction in a desert city like Las Vegas, and has become more so in the fifteen years since I invented the Goliath's Hotel's interior waterway—my husband named it the Love Moat—for the Quartet. An old-time carnival tunnel of love ride also shows up in the Quartet, and in different form as both a dangerous place of mystery and man/woman relationships in the later *Cat in a Diamond Dazzle*. That's another reason I'm glad to see the Quartet back in print: its many links to your later adventures.

By the way, Louie, I notice you have the usual masculine tendency to pooh-pooh romances, no doubt because you miss seeing the underlying feminist content.

Huh? The only underlying content I want to see in my books is feline. I do not get it with you humans and the propagation of the species. We cats make it simple and short: Twice a year the female is seized by raging hormonal imbalances that make her wildly attractive to the male despite her wishes, and we dudes beat each other up for the privilege of l'amour with the proper strangers. So it goes until the moment of biological madness passes, then we all go our separate ways, the dudes satisfied and the dames with kits. What more does any species want or need? Though I do see why we need human help in universally curtailing our activities because of the huge overpopulation problem resulting in poverty and assorted miseries, but you humans face the same consequences.

As usual, Louie, you have put matters in your uniquely noir style. I should mention that, thanks to ill-meant but opportune villainy in one of your regular series cases, you are now the proud possessor of a Virtual vasectomy. You can no longer contribute to the overpopulation problem, even fictionally, and have embraced your politically correct condition by regarding it as a "license to thrill." I'm afraid you'll never understand the romance mythology.

Okay. I will set myself up. What myth do we tackle in our next tome, *The Cat and the Jill of Diamonds*?

Cupid and Psyche.

Cupid I know. That's the chubby lad in a diaphanous diaper with the Robin Hood complex. Who is this Psyche? Does that mean we get a wacko in the next book?

As a matter of fact, we do, but luckily it's not any of our main characters.

Good. A wacko will make this next outing much more noir. You can never have too much noir, or *moi,* in a Midnight Louie mystery.